303351300 7

D1825589

Shannon McKenna is the
New York Times and *USA TODAY*
bestselling author of over thirty romance
novels, ranging from romantic suspense
to contemporary romance and even
to paranormal. She loves abandoning
herself to the magic of a story. Writing
her own stories is a dream come true.

She loves to hear from readers. Visit
her website, shannonmckenna.com.
Find her on Facebook at Facebook.com/
authorshannonmckenna, or join her
newsletter at shannonmckenna.com/
connect.php and look for your
welcome gift!

The Marriage Mandate

SHANNON McKENNA

MILLS & BOON

First published in Great Britain 2022
by Mills & Boon, an imprint of HarperCollins*Publishers* Ltd,
1 London Bridge Street, London, SE1 9GF

www.harpercollins.co.uk

HarperCollins*Publishers*
1st Floor, Watermarque Building,
Ringsend Road, Dublin 4, Ireland

Large Print edition 2022

The Marriage Mandate © 2022 Shannon McKenna

ISBN: 978-0-263-29685-3

09/22

MIX
Paper from
responsible sources
FSC™ C007454

This book is produced from independently certified FSC™ paper to ensure responsible forest management. For more information visit www.harpercollins.co.uk/green.

Printed and Bound in the UK using 100% Renewable Electricity at CPI Group (UK) Ltd, Croydon, CR0 4YY

One

"Take heart, girlfriend." Geri, one of Maddie Moss's good friends, lifted her mojito and clicked her glass with Maddie's. "You're in the perfect place. Trix and Terrence's wedding extravaganza is just the place for supercharged man hunting. You'll be matched up in no time."

"I'm not in the mood for man hunting," Maddie Moss said rebelliously as she frowned out at the cocktail gathering, one of the many events that were crowded into her good friend Trix's blow-out wedding weekend. "It's crass and undignified and desperate, and it's not who I am."

"Too bad for you, hon," Geri said, not without sympathy. "You don't have much of a choice, right? And shopping really can be fun. Look around yourself. What about Aston or Gabe or Richie or Herschel or Sam or Bruce?"

Maddie looked at each of the men that her friend had nominated in turn, sipped her margarita and shook her head. "Nope," she said. "They won't do."

Geri rolled her eyes impatiently. "For a woman under constraint, you're very persnickety. Your grandma said that the rule was, married by your thirtieth birthday, which is in a couple of months. And not just engaged, but full-on married. Am I right? Weddings take time to plan, and you still don't have a groom. Tick tock, tick tock."

"Believe me, I'm hyperaware of my timeline," Maddie muttered. "And of the penalties for missing it."

"Oh, stop complaining. This wedding is a veritable eligible bachelor buffet. And just as a backup, next week you've also got Ava Maddox's wedding to attend. So if you don't get lucky here, you get another shot there. I mean, just look at them, arrayed before you in all their glory, peacock tails spread out. Aston's very smart, and he's going to inherit Hollis Breweries. And Gabe has great abs. Didn't you see them at the beach, earlier today?"

"Couldn't have missed them if I wanted to," Maddie said. "Gabe makes sure that everyone sees his abs."

"Not a single one of them is bad looking," Geri persisted. "And some are pretty handsome. Sam's good-looking, so are Aston and Richie. Bruce is an up-and-coming DA. Herschel just got hired as chief operating officer at some new electronics company. It's not a bad lineup, Maddie. Keep your mind open, okay?"

"I know these guys too well, Geri. Aston is an arrogant asshat. I had dinner with him once, and he yelled into his phone for the entire meal. Sam can't talk about anything but sports. Richie mansplains math theory to me whenever we talk—"

"Oh, God forbid," Geri murmured. "Math theory? To the math goddess herself? Hasn't he been warned?"

"Apparently not," Maddie said. "Herschel is afraid of me, which gets boring really fast. Gabe is like an overexcited Labrador puppy, plus, he can't seem to keep his shirt buttoned over his six-pack."

"That leaves Bruce," Geri encouraged. "He's aggressive, ambitious. A go-getter."

"Yeah, he definitely goes out and gets a whole

lot of everything," Maddie said dryly. "Hilary dumped him four months ago because he gave her chlamydia."

Geri sighed and took a sip of her drink. "Well, damn, girl. Nobody's perfect." Her eyes sharpened, focusing over Maddie's shoulder. "Wait. I take that back." Her voice had lowered to an awestruck whisper. "I just saw perfection in human form. One of Terrence's out-of-town groomsmen who couldn't make it to the rehearsal dinner last night. I spotted him when he got out of his cab from the airport. Trix said he was one of Terrence's old friends, some science genius who lives abroad. He has an amazing ass, among his many other magnificent attributes. Lord save us."

Maddie turned to look, her curiosity piqued.

She froze as pure panic made her whole body vibrate like a plucked string. Her mind went blank.

Jack Daly? *He* was one of Terrence's groomsmen? And he was going to be in the wedding party, along with her? Oh, dear God.

It hardly seemed possible, but after nine years, the man was even more gorgeous than she remembered. He looked tougher. He was casually dressed, in loose tan pants and a white linen shirt, open at the throat, showing a sliver of deeply tanned chest. He had a tall, rangy body. Broad shoulders, long legs, huge hands, a square jaw. She'd always loved his hooked nose. Intense, deep-set dark brown eyes under a heavy slash of dark eyebrows. He was more heavily muscled than she remembered, his face harder.

Maddie whipped her head back around as Jack's gaze flicked toward her.

Geri looked puzzled. "You okay? Your face looks flushed. Is it the hottie? He certainly made my temperature spike. Whew! Be still, my heart."

"I know that guy," she admitted.

"Omigod, really?" Geri's eyes sparkled. "Will you introduce me?"

"No! Absolutely no, Geri. He's bad news. The absolute worst. Total nightmare. Put him out of your mind and lock the door."

Geri's very red lips fell open for a moment. Then she leaned forward across the table, bright-eyed. "Yum. Scandal, eh? Tell me everything!"

"It's not like that, Geri," Maddie said. "It's not fun, hot, juicy scandal. It's sad, awful, stupid scandal. No fun at all."

"Well, I'm still curious," Geri prodded. "Come on. Deliver the goods."

Maddie blew out a frustrated breath, her heart still thumping far too fast. "Fine, if you must know. You know my brother Caleb, of course."

"Of course. Every straight woman with a pulse knows your brother Caleb," Geri said. "We're all devastated that he's been taken off the market. What about him?"

"Caleb and Jack Daly were best friends, back in high school," Maddie said. "They were also roommates at Stanford. After college, they launched a start-up together, called BioSpark. Enzymatic recycling. They grew microbes that produced enzymes that could digest and break down plastic waste at accelerated rates in landfills and the ocean. They'd developed this product, Carbon Clean. Everyone was excited about it. They were just about to go public, and make a real killing."

Geri made an appreciative sound in her throat. "Mmm. So Jack Daly has a brain behind that pretty face, too? It hardly seems fair."

"It's not funny, Geri," Maddie said sharply. "He screwed my brother over. Caleb can't definitively prove that Jack leaked the research to Energen, one of their competitors, but the evidence all points to it. And it's a proven fact that Jack secretly invested seven hundred thousand dollars in Energen stock right before Energen went public, days before BioSpark's IPO. Word got out, and BioSpark's IPO tanked. And Jack went to jail."

"Oh," Geri murmured, crestfallen. "Bummer. What a waste of a delicious man."

"He got out on a technicality six months later, which drove Caleb absolutely crazy," Maddie went on. "But that's who we're dealing with, Geri. A lying, cheating, backstabbing criminal. Leave that guy alone."

"Hmm." Geri studied Jack, eyes bright with speculation. "Strange. Wouldn't he have made more money eventually if he'd just stayed the course with his own company?"

"We all certainly thought so, sure, but who knows how his twisted reasoning went," Maddie said. "Of course, he told everyone he'd been set up, blah-blah-blah, but the evidence against him was overwhelming."

"Strange," Geri murmured again.

Maddie steeled herself not to look. "Please stop staring at him, Ger. You'll draw his attention to us."

"I'm sorry, but I can't. Physiologically, I simply can't. So why would he do it?"

"I doubt we'll ever know. Caleb and Gran figured he must have been jealous."

"Of what? Didn't they open their company together, as equal partners? And equally handsome, too. What stunning foils for each other they must have been. Mmm."

"Jealous of our family background," Maddie explained. "Our upbringing. I mean, I never knew my parents, and Caleb and Marcus just barely remember our mom, but Gran and Grandpa Bertram were always there for us. We had everything we needed in life to do well, and Jack just…didn't. His dad was killed in a work accident when Jack was just a teenager, and he ended up in foster care. So it was pretty miraculous that he did so well in school. Great grades, great test scores, full ride at Stanford, et cetera, et cetera. But evidently all that trauma left its mark. Some stuff only comes out over time, under pressure."

Geri's eyes went big and soft as she sucked up her drink with her straw, rattling the ice cubes. "Aw," she murmured, "that's so sad."

"Don't you dare feel sorry for him!" Maddie hissed. "He messed up my big brother! It really cut Caleb to the heart. He was never the same afterward."

"I'm sorry for Caleb, too, but damn, how can

I help feeling sorry for Jack? It's your own fault, Mads. The way you told the story tugged my heartstrings."

"Well, pull your heartstrings loose because you're not getting anywhere near Jack Daly, if I have anything to say about it."

Geri rolled her eyes. "C'mon, Mads. Agreed, he was a bad boy. Agreed, he did a bad thing. But it was nine years ago, right? He paid his debt to society. And he's a total dreamboat. And he must be scary smart, to go into business with a Moss."

"Sure, he's smart. Genius level. Didn't do him much good, did it?"

Geri rested her chin on her clasped hands, studying her friend with interest. "My, my," she said thoughtfully. "So passionate. It's refreshing, after seeing you mope around for months since this marriage mandate nonsense popped up. You have color in your cheeks. Your eyes are spar-kling. Intriguing, Mads."

Her tone got Maddie's back up. Geri just re-fused to grasp the gravity of Jack Daly's crimes. "Do you blame me for being passionate about this?" she demanded.

"Not at all," Geri soothed. "But you'll be stand-ing up at the altar with this guy at the wedding, if he's Terrence's groomsman. The wedding pictures will have you guys together, plastered all over social media. Awkward."

"Caleb will go ballistic," Maddie said grimly. "He'd rip Jack's head off if he ever saw him. Gran, too. Elegantly, of course, but he'd still end up headless."

"Really." Geri's eyes narrowed thoughtfully. "Honey. I sense an opportunity here."

"How so? I see a big, messy problem."

"Consider this," Geri said. "You need a raw force of nature, powerful enough to push back against your grandma. Could Jack Daly be that force?"

Maddie's body tightened up at Geri's vague, oblique suggestion and its dangerous implications. "What on earth are you talking about?"

"I don't know yet," Geri said. "I'm just feeling my way. But you seem to be stuck, Mads. Maybe, somehow, the powerful emotions elicited by this Jack Daly could be useful to you somehow. I'm just throwing it out there, you know? Chew on it."

"I am bewildered, babe," Maddie told her.

"I get that a lot," Geri said serenely. "In any case, it could be entertaining. I mean, he's gorgeous. Why not bop him around a little?"

"Because he has no conscience? Because he screwed my brother over?"

"I never said you had to marry him, Mads, or even let him near the good silver. You could just use him for your own wicked, selfish purposes. Pretend to get involved with him. Scare your grandma to death with him. God knows, she deserves it, for jerking you around like this."

"Are you actually suggesting that I…holy crap. You're joking."

"Of course I am, honey," Geri said lightly. "But there's a little bit of truth in every joke. And be straight with me. When Caleb brought that stunning Adonis home for Sunday dinners and spring breaks and summer barbecues—you thought about it." Geri read Maddie's face and nodded sagely. "C'mon. You looked covetously upon his male beauty. Fess up."

"Well, yes," Maddie said defensively. "Of course I crushed on him. But he never even noticed me. I was just the geeky little sister with the braces and the glasses and the bad hair."

Geri gave Maddie an assessing look, and made a low, purring sound of approval in her throat. "Well, not anymore, hmm? You're all grown-up, and smokin' hot. I love that blue halter dress.

Does great things for the girls. Not that they need any help."

"Thanks," Maddie said graciously. "The girls thank you, too. And you're looking pretty fine yourself, in that little yellow number. Nice choice."

Geri preened, adjusting her blond curls. "I try," she said demurely. "Just let me know if you decide to make that guy a part of your strategy to wiggle out of your Gran's mandate. Because if he's not otherwise engaged, I just might take him for a whirl this weekend myself."

"Don't!" Maddie burst out. "Promise me you won't, Geri."

Geri blinked innocently. "Wow. The emotional intensity just gives me chills."

"Not at all," Maddie said, her voice grimly controlled. "But that guy is toxic. He would be toxic for you, too. So please. Don't."

"Ah, sweet, sweet poison." Geri leaned her chin on her hand and gazed longingly across the room toward Jack Daly. "Maybe just a little, bitty taste?"

Unable to resist any longer, Maddie dared a quick peek of her own. Jack was at the bar, talking to Terrence, the future bridegroom. He took a pull off his beer, and then glanced out around the room. Their eyes met, and she whipped her gaze away, but not before a shudder of physical awareness had jolted her whole body.

And Geri's sharp blue eyes saw it all. "Well, get out there and mingle," she said. "I'll give you some time to ponder this indecent suggestion, and then, I start making some indecent suggestions of my own. Because life is short—but I am betting that guy is *not*."

Maddie flushed again. "Geri! Did you hear nothing that I said?"

"Wow, honey. If I didn't know better, I'd say you were almost possessive."

"Geri, please stop it," Maddie said through her teeth.

Geri's lips twitched. "Okay, I'll be good," she soothed. "Don't worry about me. Go on. Get out there, Mads. You've got a husband to find. Happy hunting."

Maddie tried to stop it, but her eyes kept being drawn back to Jack Daly.

He was a liar. A thief. A traitor to his friends. She had to repeat that litany of his deadly sins to herself, over and over again.

Until it finally took.

Jack couldn't figure the mystery woman out. She was a jaw-dropping bombshell. Ice-blue halter dress, luscious curves, pale brown skin, a crown of wild black ringlets, fabulous lips. One of the prettiest women he's ever seen. Something about her was familiar, but no way could he forget a face like that. Lips like that, painted with a plum-colored gloss. Just a glance made him break out in a sweat.

She wouldn't look at him. Unlike the sultry blonde at the table with her, who had stared fixedly. Then again, a woman as pretty as the one in the blue dress would have trained herself to avoid eye contact, like a waiter in a busy restaurant. He'd been a waiter, so he knew good and well that the only way through a bustling dining room was to keep eyes strictly forward.

She looked his way for a split second—and then whipped her gaze away as a bolt of horrified recognition zinged through him.

Oh, yeah. He knew that girl. That was Maddie Moss. Caleb Moss's little sister.

She looked completely different than he remembered. Sure, she'd been cute, back in the day, but he and Caleb had been distracted with their big plans, and busy with their high-energy lives, and they had largely ignored her when they came across her. Little Mads, with the metal-mouth and the glasses, all knees and elbows and smart remarks.

Well, goddamn. She was a stunner now.

"Everything okay, man?" Terrence, the bride-groom-to-be, waved his hand in front of Jack's face. "Did you see a ghost?"

"No. The bombshell in the light blue dress," Jack told him.

"Whoo, yeah." Terrence whistled apprecia-tively. "Good taste. Trix had to really struggle to decide if she wanted to have a bridesmaid that good-looking. The bride doesn't want to get shown up by her bridesmaids, you know? But she liked Maddie so much, she decided it was worth it. She's definitely the hottest in the pack. Want me to pull strings to get her next to you in the procession? And at the reception? I could swing that."

"She's one of Trix's bridesmaids?" Jack's voice cracked with horror.

Terrence's eyes narrowed. "Uh…and this is so terrible why, exactly? I thought you'd be psyched. I mean, look at her. Who can object to that?"

"You remember my troubles nine years ago with Caleb Moss?"

"Sure," Terrence said. "But I also know that

you're innocent, and so does everyone else with half a brain. What about it?"

"I appreciate your vote of confidence," Jack said, meaning it with all his heart. "But Maddie Moss is Caleb's sister."

Terrence's eyes widened with shock. "Oh, shit!" He turned to look in Maddie's direction. "But she doesn't look like she could be Caleb's sister. She's biracial, right? Is she, what, adopted, or something?"

"No. Different dads. Their brother Marcus has a different dad, too. Asian. But they're all Mosses. And they all collectively hate my guts."

"Damn, Jack. That totally sucks. I'm really sorry we did this to you. Do you think that she'll make a thing of it? That it'll be a problem?"

"Couldn't tell you," Jack said. "I haven't seen her for nine years, and back then, she was just a kid, so that's a big question mark. She definitely recognized me. She's ignoring me now." Jack stared out into the crowd. "The smart thing would be for me to pull out of the wedding party. Ask someone else to be your fourth groomsman, and I'll revert to being a normal guest, ready to scram if things get complicated."

"Hell, no." Terrence's voice was sharp. "I let Trix have her way about every detail of this wed-

ding, but I'll be damned if you won't stand up
with me when I take my vows. You're the only
reason I got through college, man. What happened with BioSpark was a disgrace. If the Moss
chick gets her back up, she can be the one to
scram. Not you."

"Don't get mad at her for something she hasn't
done yet," Jack soothed.

Terrence tossed back the last swallow of beer.
"Trix is signaling me. Time to mobilize for the
bonfire cookout on the beach. You'll be there?"

"I'll be there," Jack assured him. "Sorry I
couldn't make the rehearsal dinner last night.
Hey, your lady beckons. Don't make her wait."

Terrence headed straight for Trix, a skinny
redhead with a toothy smile. She was a nervous
wreck, but she was a bubbly, happy nervous
wreck, and Terrence doted on her.

Terrence was a great guy. Jack was deeply
grateful for that small but precious handful of
old friends who had stuck by him after the Bio-
Spark disaster. He'd had an impossible time finding work in his field after that. No one wanted to
hire a person who had been accused of passing
intellectual property to a competitor, or betting
against his own team.

He'd only started to find work in biotechnology a few years ago, thanks to the influence of some friends who had contacts in overseas companies. In the past four years, he'd worked in Asia, Hungary and South Africa. He'd been very glad to leave the long string of random jobs and work in biotechnology again, even at a lower level, with smaller budgets. He'd learned to content himself. To be grateful. Things could be so much worse.

He glanced at the table where Maddie Moss had been sitting with her blonde friend. She had slipped away, avoiding eye contact except for that one electric moment that still reverberated inside him.

It was probably no big deal. She would probably just avoid him. Pretend he didn't exist. That would be the smart thing, and Maddie had the Moss smarts.

So he would do the same. Damn. Terrence had no clue about Maddie, but Trix did, and she should have known better. This weekend was going to be tense and awkward.

Boo-hoo, poor you. It sounded like Dad's gruff voice in his head. *You know what's tense and awkward, boy? A jail cell. Stop feeling sorry for yourself.*

So his life had gotten derailed. At least he had

a life, and he was free to live it. He wasn't rotting behind bars.

Therefore, no whining allowed. Even if his efforts to work again in his chosen field fell through, he'd still be fine. He'd live. It was good to be alive.

No more dark thoughts, or else he'd turn into a black hole and suck all the air and the energy out of Trix and Terrence's party.

But it hurt to be reminded that his best friend, as well as that man's entire family, saw him as a ruthless predator. And that he was unable to prove his innocence to them.

That made him so frustrated, he wanted to explode.

Two

Maddie made a big show of having fun at the beach party. There was a gazebo set up, an open-air charcoal fire for barbecuing ribs, steaks, burgers. A table full of salads and sides, cocktails, beer and wine.

But her appetite was canceled out by her intense awareness of Jack Daly.

Not that he got anywhere near her, or even noticed that she was there. Maybe he hadn't recognized her. He was busy laughing and flirting with Oksana, a stunning blonde Russian model. Trix worked at a big modeling agency, so a large number of her female friends were very tall, slim and unnaturally good-looking.

Oksana was putting her perfectly manicured hand on his arm, clutching him to steady herself. As well she should, in those ridiculous shoes. What was she thinking, going to a beach party in spike heels and a skintight sheath dress?

Oksana gulped her champagne spritzer and squealed as her ankles wobbled, grabbing Jack again for support.

Don't count on him, girl. He will let you fall. You'll hit the ground so hard.

Maddie was sick of watching it, so she grabbed an eco-plastic cup of champagne spritzer from the bar, kicked off her sandals and strolled off toward the water to sip it in blessed solitude.

The beach was gorgeous. It was a beautiful night. Chilly, as always, and there was cloud cover, but she'd changed into her sweatshirt and her cut-off jeans for the beach. She dug her feet into the cold wet sand as she walked toward the white foamy water rushing over the sand.

The moon glowed behind the clouds, making an eerie halo. The noise of the party and the crackle of the big bonfire retreated into the distance as the sand got soggier. She gasped with startled delight as the icy water swirled suddenly over her feet.

The deep, pulsing roar of the ocean was so cleansing. *Ahhh.*

"And what are you doing out here, off on your own in the dark?"

She turned to look. Bruce Traynor had followed her. And so it began.

"Hey, Bruce," she said politely, glad it was dark enough so she didn't have to fake a smile. Small mercies.

Bruce jerked back when the icy water washed over his feet. "Shit!"

Maddie stifled a giggle as Bruce scrambled back out of the water.

"Well?" he said. "Aren't you going to join me over here? My shoes are soaked."

Maddie glanced down at Bruce's expensive canvas boat shoes. What kind of guy wore shoes like that to a beach? He should hook up with Oksana. Those two would understand each other.

"I came barefoot on purpose," she told him. "I love to wade in the water."

Bruce hesitated for a moment, and then slogged grimly through the sand toward her. "Fine, if you have to make a thing of it," he grumbled.

"It's not a thing," Maddie murmured. "I'm just enjoying the waves."

Bruce gasped as water rushed over his feet

once again. "God, that's cold. So I've been meaning to talk to you, but you're always in a crowd.
Bees flocking to honey, and all that. Who can
blame them, when it's so sweet."

"I'm not sweet, Bruce." *Not to you, anyway.*

"I beg to differ." Bruce's teeth flashed. "This
thing with your grandmother. Is it true, this news
going around? That you need to get married by...
when, exactly?"

"My thirtieth birthday," she said, with grim
resignation. "September."

"So you're a Virgo? My mom's a Virgo, too.
You guys would get along."

"Would we?" Maddie had heard gruesome
tales of Bruce's control freak mother from Hilary, Bruce's disgruntled ex-fiancée.

"Absolutely. I'm going to get right to the point,
since there's no time to waste—"

"Let me stop you right there, Bruce—"

"I have to get this off my chest. I've admired
you for years, Maddie. I have to tell you—"

"I don't want to hear it," Maddie said swiftly.

But Bruce wasn't listening. "This may seem
out of the blue," he continued, raising his voice
over her attempts to speak. "But in our social
circles, we have to take a more pragmatic view

of things. Dynasties joining, fortunes uniting. The fate of nations, you know?"

"Fate of nations?" She turned her bark of laughter into a stifled cough. "That may be over-stating things a little."

"Not at all," Bruce said loftily. "People like us can't afford to be jerked around by romantic fantasies, or unrealistic societal ideals. And if you need a husband to preserve the family fortune? I stand ready. I offer up my services."

"For real, Bruce?" She coughed again. "You want to...service me?"

"Absolutely. I'd be honored. I've thought it through very carefully, looking at every angle, and I've decided that it's really the best thing for both of us."

"Aw," Maddie murmured. "So you've thought it through for me as well as for yourself. Wow, Bruce. That's really generous of you."

"My pleasure." Bruce missed the irony in her tone completely. "I stand ready to help with all your important decisions, as your partner and husband. Think about it, Maddie. It's truly the perfect solution for all your problems. And just in time, too."

"Well, try not to take this personally, but I

don't feel that way about you," Maddie said. "I don't want to marry you, Bruce, because I—"

"You don't love me," Bruce finished matter-of-factly. "Of course not. I don't love you, either. It's not necessary, or even relevant. It's much smarter to make choices based on reality. Practicality. Like they did in the olden days."

"In the olden days, women were chattel," Maddie reminded him. "They had no say at all in who they married. So believe me, I am not nostalgic for the olden days."

"You are deliberately missing my point," Bruce snapped. "You have no time to waste, with your grandmother demanding that you get married, and I'm offering you a ready-made solution. I've always thought girls' insistence on romantic love was silly. Love is just lust in a fancy costume, after all. God knows, I'm in lust with you. As far as I'm concerned, mutual respect, honesty, an iron-clad prenup and a healthy dose of lust? That's more than good enough for me." He grabbed her hand and jerked her toward him.

Maddie yanked back, trying to pull it free. "That's not the case for me," she said sharply. "Because I'm not in lust with you."

"How would you know?" Bruce jerked her closer, and kissed her.

Maddie lost her balance, the sand shifting beneath her feet as a wave receded. Icy water sucked and dragged at her ankles. Bruce's smothering kiss tasted like wine and onions. His teeth nicked her lip, his tongue probed, slimy and revolting.

Maddie turned her head away, gasping for air. She struggled to free herself, shoving at him. "What the hell do you think you're doing?"

"Giving you a taste." Bruce's voice was an oily ticklish buzz in her ear. "Just relax. Let me show you how good it could be."

Maddie hauled off and landed a stinging slap to his cheek.

Bruce rocked back, his eyes big with shock. "What?" he squawked. "What in the hell is wrong with you? I was offering you marriage!"

"And I was saying 'no,'" she told him crisply. "You weren't listening."

Bruce sputtered helplessly. "But...but do you have any idea what you're turning down? I was willing to overlook your family history—"

"Family history? What family history are you referring to?"

"I was offering you the Traynor family name!" he yelled. "Which is a hell of a lot more than your father offered your mother, from the stories I've heard! And you just throw it right back in my face, like it's nothing?"

"No, I'm throwing *this.*" Maddie flung her spritzer into his face.

Bruce stumbled back. His mouth hung open, working helplessly as he wiped his face.

"My mother did exactly as she pleased," Maddie told him. "In that, I take after her. I'm not your girl. Give it up."

"Is everything okay here?"

Maddie spun around at that deep, quiet voice behind her. Jack Daly stood there, his dark eyes alert and attentive. Watching everything.

"We're fine," Bruce snarled, wiping his face. "Move along. Nothing to see here."

"I was asking her, not you," Jack said calmly.

"Get lost, Daly! She doesn't need anything from a thieving jailbird loser like you."

"She doesn't need anything from you, either, from what I could tell. How about you just go, before the situation degenerates any further. You get me?"

Bruce glared at Maddie as he backed away. "You're going to regret this."

"I'll run that risk. Good night, Bruce."

Bruce slogged away through the sand, muttering furiously to himself.

Leaving just her and Jack Daly standing there in the moonlight alone, the ocean waves surging and retreating around them.

"Are you okay?" Jack asked again.

"Fine," she said.

"That guy's a dickhead. Are you sure you're—"

"I'm fine," she repeated. "I didn't need to be rescued, either. Certainly not by you. Bruce isn't dangerous. He's just a jerk."

Understood," Jack said. "What's that thing he said, about your grandmother insisting on marriage?"

"My issues with my family are none of your damn business."

"No, I guess not. I'll just go ask around. I'll get the public gossip version."

Maddie snorted. "Oh, please. All right, to put it briefly, Gran has decided to blackmail all of us into getting married. No carrot, all stick. And the stick is, if we fail to deliver her a legal spouse by the stipulated date, she hands her controlling shares of MossTech over to my pompous, greedy, dumbass uncle Jerome. He'll take MossTech public as fast as he can, and that will be the end of MossTech as we know it."

Jack was silent for a long moment. "That would be a shame."

"Of course, Gran's mandate worked out fine for Caleb," she said. "He got lucky, when Tilda blew back into his life with their kid, Annika. She's just the cutest little girl. Do you remember Tilda?"

"Of course," Jack said. "Tilda had a kid? I didn't know that."

"Neither did we, but she's the best thing that ever happened to us," she said. "Annika is a Moss, through and through. We love her to pieces. But now that Caleb came through with flying colors, Gran got even more fired up, and now she's pressuring me. I turn thirty in less than three months, and that's my cut-off point. Thirty-five for the boys, but thirty for me because I'm female, and my eggs are getting stale, evidently. Word has gotten out, so all the opportunistic slime-bags are coming at me, right and left. The Moss fortune is very motivating, you know? It inspires great passion in many men."

"Maybe it's you they want," he suggested.

"Nope, I have no illusions there," she said glumly. "It's MossTech they want, not me. Which is demoralizing as hell. The worst possible conditions for husband hunting. Who can find the right needle in a haystack of gold-digging assholes? I can't even find someone decent to spend a Saturday night with. Let alone forge a lifetime commitment."

It was hard to tell in the moonlight, but Jack seemed to be looking her over, from her bare, sandy toes all the way up to her wind-tossed hair.

"I can't imagine you having that much trouble with it," he said.

She snorted. "Imagine again. The obvious solution is just to not comply. Just let whatever happens happen, and then see what life offers afterward. I could do without MossTech. I could open my own forensic accounting consultancy, and get more work than I can handle. I'd be fine. Maybe even happier, in the long run."

"Forensic accounting?" Jack sounded startled. "Really?"

"Yeah. I've always been a number geek. Is it so hard to believe?"

"Yeah, but those words conjure up guys in glasses with paunches and comb-overs, staring at screens until their eyes bug out. I don't picture...well...you know." He gestured in her general direction. "You."

"I have the glasses," she assured him. "I love my glasses. And I stare at screens until my eyes look like stoplights. But believe it or not, yeah, that's my jam. Wallowing in numbers. Finding patterns in data. Running statistics. I love it. More than I would love being a C-suite executive at MossTech. But Gran's got this thing, about concentrating all the family talent in MossTech. She wants me to be the chief financial officer."

"Damn," Jack said. "No one could say that's not a brilliant career move."

She shrugged. "Sure, but if I don't find someone to marry in the next few weeks, Uncle Jerome takes control and fires us all anyway. So it's all, well. Pointless."

"Ouch," Jack murmured.

"I'd be fine. I wouldn't mind working without my family breathing down my neck. But Jerome would fire Caleb and Marcus, too, and that's a huge shame. And of course, MossTech would go over to the dark side. At least, the way we see it."

"That would suck," he agreed.

"Yes. Gran counts on familial guilt to control us. But that doesn't make husband hunting easier. What am I supposed to do, marry an asshat like Bruce just to be compliant? That would kill me. And Gran herself would get sick of a guy like him in ten minutes flat. She's asking the impossible."

"Absolutely don't marry someone like Bruce," Jack said forcefully.

"Hell, no. I will not flush my life down the toilet to please anybody. But if I can't find anyone I like in time, I blow up MossTech and destroy my brothers' careers, and that makes me miserable. Though eventually they'll be fine. Knowing them."

Knowing them. That reminded her abruptly that Jack did indeed know them. He knew all of them. All too well.

Panic gripped her. What the hell was she thinking? Babbling family problems to this man, of all people? Jack Daly was not her confidant. He was the enemy.

"How about a third option?" Jack asked.

That startled her out of her mini panic. "I don't see any third option."

"Get your grandmother to relent," he said.

"Ha! You've met Gran. Have you ever seen her relent? Or admit she was wrong?"

Jack grunted under his breath. "You have a point. So strong-arm her into it. Scare her. Bring home someone whose guts she will hate. Fight fire with fire."

Someone whose guts she will hate. A thief, a traitor. A corporate spy. A jailbird.

The excitement flashing through her at that fleeting thought scared her to death.

"I shouldn't talk about my family to you." Her voice had a quaver that she couldn't control. "I shouldn't be talking to you at all."

"Probably not," he said. "But here we are."

Maddie was right. He should back off and leave her be. Right…freaking…*now.*

But she was so pretty in the light of the moon. Her big, gorgeous eyes gleamed in the moonlight. And those lips. God, how could he have never noticed those lips?

Because he'd been dazzled by Gabriella Adriani back then. His ex.

It had been a long time since he'd thought about Gabriella. Nine years ago, he'd thought himself in love with her. Gabriella was beautiful, sexy, smart, full of attitude.

But she'd bailed on him when things went bad with BioSpark. He'd nursed hurt feelings for quite some time, but in the end, he didn't blame her. Gabriella had big plans for her life, and a fiancé as compromised as he was would have been a heavy load to drag.

It was odd, but right now, looking at Maddie Moss in those ripped cut-off jeans, he couldn't even remember what Gabriella looked like. The loose, slouchy sweatshirt did not manage to hide the deep sexy curves of Maddie's body. She looked as fine in that casual getup as she had in the stunning halter dress. It made his lower body tighten and thrum.

No, no, no. Not the place, not the time, not the woman. Don't, Daly.

Maddie must have sensed the hungry energy blasting off him, because she backed away. "So, um...bye."

She walked away quickly. Her mass of springy black ringlets bounced sexily with every step. Her footprints were narrow, distinct. Dainty, even.

Though she was hardly dainty. He grinned, remembering how she'd smacked that horse's ass, Bruce Traynor, and tossed a drink in his smirking face.

He wished he'd filmed it for posterity. Maddie Moss, being badass.

He needed to shut this fantasy down, and stay as far away from her as possible. Preferably in a different room. A different state would be even better.

As he walked back to the bonfire, he was hyperaware of Maddie's location in the crowd of partygoers, as if she were lit up by a spotlight that followed her around wherever she went. A crowd of men literally did follow her around. There were at least five of them clustered around her at any given moment: one pouring her champagne, one setting up a folding chair for her to sit down, one bringing her a plate of assorted Italian pastries.

They were totally swarming her, but she managed them easily and graciously. Chatting and laughing politely at their jokes. Pleasant with all of them, favoring none.

There must be scores of men who would go to any desperate lengths just to have a cup of coffee with her, let alone marry her. The idea of getting to see all that elusive, complicated, dangerous, alluring femininity up close…wow.

Look away. You have no margin for error, boy. Dad's voice. once again.

At least, Bruce Traynor wasn't in the swarm. He was on the opposite side of the bonfire, looking damp, sticky and bad-tempered. Traynor glowered at Jack, who grinned back at him, and lifted his beer.

Eat it, bonehead. At least that jackass was out of the running.

Scary, how much satisfaction that fact gave him.

"Hey, dude."

Jack turned to see Gabe Morehead standing there, his denim shirt hanging open to show his deeply bronzed six-pack, and lots of tribal man jewelry on leather cords, featuring shark teeth, bear claws and runic medallions. "Hey, Gabe. What's up?"

"Did I see Maddie Moss talking to you? Was she, what, chewing you out?"

"Just pleasantries," Jack said.

"Pleasantries, my ass. I bet she was biting your head off. I can't believe Trix invited both of you to the wedding. What a gaffe."

"Terrence and I go way back," Jack offered.

"Ah." Gabe sucked on his beer, gazing across the bonfire in Maddie's direction. "Well, at least we don't have to compete with you, on top of everything else. Man, that woman is fine. Look at those legs. Love to have 'em wrapped around my waist while I—".

"Stick a sock in it, Gabe," Jack cut in.

Gabe looked startled. "Oh! So it's like that, huh?"

"Nah. Just not in the mood for your sexual fantasies."

"Okay," Gabe said. "But I wouldn't blame you if you had a crush on her. The woman is a force of nature. Filthy rich, too. And she has brains that just won't quit. Darrell and Frederick had some problems in their accounting department, and they called her in a couple months ago. They told me that she set up a room and worked in there with her computer and a bunch of whiteboards for a few days. Then she came out and told them exactly where the problem was. Who, when, where, how much, down to the penny. They confronted the thief, and he admitted everything. They say she nailed every last detail. They were awestruck."

"Is that so," Jack said.

"Yeah, genius level magic, man. She charged them an arm and a leg, but it was worth it. Shame she hates your guts. If you really were framed in that BioSpark thing, then she'd be the person you'd want to comb through the rubble for you. She's got brains to burn. But you win some, you lose some, right? I'm getting another beer. Want one?"

"No, I'm good," Jack said.

As if she felt his gaze, Maddie turned her head and looked at him. The eye contact made everything inside him light up.

He looked away swiftly. He had to at least try not to be a creeper.

Bad luck and trouble had put Maddie Moss out

of his reach forever. But it was hard to swallow. A smart, gorgeous, desirable woman, shrinking away from him because she thought he was a lying scumbag, thief and traitor.

He'd worked hard over the years to get a grip on his emotions. To always keep his cool, deliberately not thinking about certain things, or giving in to certain feelings. Or else the unfairness of it would've driven him over the edge.

But the injustice really got to him sometimes. Hell, if he'd torpedoed his own life out of greed or spite or lust, or something dumb and selfish like that, then fair enough. He'd take his medicine like a man because he would have deserved it.

But he hadn't deserved it.

It was like being under a curse. It was particularly ironic, if Maddie Moss happened to be the one with the secret sauce. The numbers whiz who might actually be able to discern the truth.

But she despised him so much, she would never get close enough to see it.

Three

Maddie was stressed and rattled at the wedding reception. Three days of bridal events had worn her out. The rehearsal dinner, the brunch buffet, the evening cocktails, the beach party. And ever since Jack Daly arrived, all her energy was taken up carefully avoiding him on the one hand, and fending off would-be suitors with the other.

Now, to put the finishing touch on her discomfort, Louis, the groomsman who was supposed to walk down the aisle with her, had pulled a last-minute switcheroo during the ceremony, when she couldn't protest. He'd grabbed the arm of Desiree, another of Trix's bridesmaids, leaving her paired up with...drumroll please... Jack Daly.

So Maddie had walked down the aisle after Trix and Terrence on Jack Daly's arm.

Then, at the reception, she'd found that Louis had switched out Jack's name card at the table next to Desiree with his own, so he could continue his flirtation. Sneaky bastard.

Jack leaned to murmur in her ear. "Don't worry," he said. "This is stupid. I don't want to put you on the spot. I'll find another place to sit. There has to be an empty chair."

"No, don't," she said swiftly. "Terrence will expect his groomsmen to be near him, for the toasts and the roasts. I really don't want to stress them. Let it be. We'll survive."

"But we'll be photographed together," he warned.

"We already have been," she pointed out. "Whatever. The fallout will play out in another time and place, so screw it. Just smile and wave."

He obliged her. That stunning smile made her breath catch in her chest. God. It just wasn't right. He looked so gorgeous in his well-cut suit. But people kept staring, smirking and whispering. People had not forgotten what happened with BioSpark.

After a while, the reception took on a surreal quality. The champagne was cold and fizzy and good. The appetizers were tantalizing, but she was too wound up to eat, not with Jack Daly close enough to her that she could smell his after-shave. Which was sweet and warm, with woodsy, tangy notes and a seductive hint of cloves. She was also close enough to admire the sharp points of his strong jaw. His close shave. The bump on his nose.

"More champagne?" he asked.

She didn't have the presence of mind to refuse. She stuck out her glass, and took another sip of the sparkling wine.

A romantic song began to play, and Terrence and Trix headed out onto the dance floor. It was a song by Moon Cat and the Kinky Ladies, a favorite band of hers.

Trix beckoned imperiously to her brides-maids. "Come on, girls!" she shouted. "Get out and dance! This is not a suggestion! Everyone in that bridesmaid dress had better get her butt out here and start shaking it, because I wield bridal power tonight!"

"Same goes for the dudes!" Terrence called out. "On your feet!"

Trix wrapped her arms around Terrence's neck and pulled his face down for a blissed out kiss as they melded into a clinch, swaying to the music.

Maddie looked desperately over toward where Louis was seated with Desiree, across the table. "Hey," she called. "Louis? Would you mind…"

Her voice trailed off, as Louis, ignoring her completely, hustled out onto the dance floor, dragging a blushing, giggling Desiree behind him. "I guess not," she concluded.

The others were partnered up, swaying to the music. Two of the groomsmen happened to already be engaged to two of the bridesmaids, so there were no odd men out.

"You don't have to do this, you know," Jack said quietly. "Pretend you sprained your ankle. Or would you rather I sprained mine? It's all the same to me."

"Hell with it. I'm compromised no matter what I do. We might as well dance." She tossed back her champagne. "Come on. Let's do this."

"Wow," he murmured. "Go easy on that stuff."

"I can handle myself. I'm a grown-up."

"I know, but you haven't eaten. You need food to soak up that much champagne."

"I can manage my own self, thanks," she told him. "And it's really creepy that you're paying close enough attention to notice."

"Sorry," he said. "Didn't mean to creep. You should still eat something."

Louis and Desiree swayed by, kissing and nuzzling as they danced.

Maddie sniffed her disapproval. "I'm surprised those two are still vertical."

"Let's not stand in the way of true love," Jack said.

"True love, my butt. Desiree's living with Hector, a really nice guy who is off in Southeast Asia right now helping set up a new micropropagation lab, and Louis is engaged to Sylvia, an economist whose working at a think tank outside of Cambridge. This is purely extracurricular fun for these two cheating airheads."

"Ah." He spun her around, and her swirling skirt wrapped itself possessively around his knees for a second before it fell free. "While the cat's away, hmm?"

"God forbid I end up married to someone who thinks I'm the cat who has to be away before the fun can start," Maddie said. "It's hard not to judge, in my current mood."

"Most people don't even try," Jack commented. "Not to judge, I mean. Judging is like breathing, for most people."

"I guess you would know." The words flew out before she'd fully vetted them.

She felt a twinge of guilt at the pained look

that flashed across his face. No need to turn the knife in the wound.

"Yeah," he said. "I do know."

Do. Not. Apologize. Goddammit. The man deserved to suffer.

They danced on in silence, but the pressure was building up inside her, and the champagne had lowered her inhibitions. "They piss me off, you know?"

"Who?" He swung her into a dip, and she flung her head back with sensual abandon. What the hell. She liked dancing, and Jack was good at it.

"Desiree and Louis," she told him, when he pulled her back up. "And I think I've figured out why. I'm jealous of them. Weirdly enough."

Jack frowned as he swung her around. "Why? What's to be jealous of? There's nothing real between them. They're empty."

"I'm jealous of people who just suit themselves. They just reach out and take what they want, without suffering agonies of guilt. And I can't do that. We had these iron-clad principles drilled into us by Gran and Grandpa Bertram, so we have this outsize sense of duty and responsibility. Then I look around, and see that other people don't have that at all. They do as they like, and to hell with the consequences. No matter who suffers."

Her face reddened. Damn. She'd done it again. Inserted her foot into her mouth as far as she could shove it. "Shit," she muttered. "Sorry."

But Jack didn't look angry. He just shook his head. "No, Maddie," he said, his voice a velvety rumble against her ear. "That's not me."

Oh, please. She'd invited him to say that. So of course, he'd obliged her. Any smooth-talking scoundrel would take an opportunity like that, if it were handed to him. She was babbling like a drunken fool. *Ooh, please, tell me that all these terrible things that I know for a fact about you aren't really true, because I don't want them to be true.*

Lie to me. Make it convincing.

She pulled back as the song ended, breaking his grip. People were swarming out onto the dance floor as the next one started.

Maddie made her way through the tables, grabbing chairs to balance herself. She grabbed a roll from a basket on the table and took a bite. Jack was right about the food. Though she hated to admit it.

"Maddie, darling!"

She turned and saw Joanna Hollis, Aston Hollis's grandmother, bearing down on her. Joanna was the Hollis matriarch, and an old frenemy of Gran's from way back.

"My dear!" she sang out. "You're just precious in that bridesmaid dress! Much prettier than the others. Most girls look hideous in a bridesmaid dress, but not a lovely morsel like you. You look just scrumptious."

Scrumptious? Morsel? She felt like a freshly caught mouse, dangling from a cat's mouth. "Hello, Mrs. Hollis. Would you excuse me? I have to—"

"Go dance with Jack Daly again?" Joanna clucked her tongue. "I don't recommend that, honey. Not one little bit."

"He's one of Terrence's groomsmen, Mrs. Hollis." She kept her voice even. "I can't avoid him. Not without making an unpleasant scene."

"I saw that dance," Joanna Hollis lectured. "Seemed like you two were having quite the animated private conversation. I can't imagine what you could have to say to such an awful man. Or what your grandmother would think of it."

"I'm sure I'll soon find out," Maddie said.

"So am I!" The older woman pinched her cheek, tittering. "You really should give my darling Aston a chance. He's my favorite grandson, you know? I know we're not supposed to have favorites, but he's such a good, smart, energetic boy."

"Mrs. Hollis, I really have to go. Please excuse—"

"You've only got a couple months left, right? With my help, we could pull off a wedding that blows this one out of the water, in time to fulfill Elaine's demands. And you could not do better than Aston. Think about it. Stay away from Jack Daly. Associating with him will taint you, and I want Aston's bride to be squeaky clean."

"Excuse me, Mrs. Hollis," she repeated, backing away into the azalea bushes.

She climbed onto one of the wooden walkways, which led her over a swampy bit of ferns and wildflowers, and onto a terrace on the other side of the resort's main building.

This terrace had a stunning view of the beach below, and Jack was standing there. Leaning on the railing and looking out at the ocean. All by himself.

Maddie's phone beeped in her evening bag. She pulled it out. Text messages from her family had piled up.

From Caleb: You're paired with Jack Daly in the wedding party? wtf?

From Tilda: call me asap. all hell is breaking loose here.

From Marcus: u have got to be freaking kidding me. have u gone nuts?

From Gran: call me immediately.

As she watched, the phone in her hand began to ring. It was Gran.

Maddie stared at it for a few moments. Then, slowly and deliberately, she declined the call and turned off the phone.

She opened up her pale green evening bag, glittering with Swarovski crystal, and dropped the phone inside. Then she marched back across the terrace toward Jack.

He sensed her approach and turned to her, his eyes wary. "Hey there," he said.

"I want to do a very dangerous thing," she blurted. "It's stupid, and wrongheaded, and probably destructive. But I want to do it anyway. And I need your help."

Jack folded his arms over his chest. "I'm listening."

"I want you to pretend to be engaged to me," she said.

For a moment, there was no expression on Jack's face at all. "Is this some kind of prank?" he finally asked.

"No," she said. "Actually, you suggested it yourself, the other night. Make Gran relent. Find someone whose guts she will hate. Scare her to death. Fight fire with fire."

"So I'm the doomsday weapon."

"Exactly. She'll be horrified, and it will serve her right, whether or not she relents. I'll still have that small satisfaction, at least."

"But this won't just drive Elaine crazy," he said. "It'll hurt Caleb, too."

Maddie felt a twinge of guilt. "Unavoidable collateral damage. He'll live."

In the silence, she suddenly sensed the depth of the pain behind the stiff mask of Jack's face, and she felt ashamed of herself, as if she'd said something wantonly cruel.

"Never mind," she said swiftly. "Sorry. Crazy idea. Let it go."

"It's no fun being your family's worst nightmare," Jack said quietly. "It's hard to get excited about it."

She took a step back. "Well, okay. I can see that this makes you miserable, so please, forget that I ever suggested it."

"I'll do it," he announced.

She was taken aback. "You...you will? But I thought—"

"On one condition."

"Ahh...there's a condition?" she said carefully. "What condition is that?"

"If you fulfill it, I'll go all out. I'll be your most embarrassing mistake. Your most egregious lapse in judgment. I'll send your family into a state of total meltdown."

"What's the condition?" she demanded again.

"So, you said you were an expert in forensic accounting, right?"

"Yes. And that is relevant exactly why?"

"I want you to go over all the data from the BioSpark implosion," he said. "I want you to help me figure out who set me up."

Four

From the blank look on Maddie's face, it was clear that she'd been expecting absolutely anything but that.

"What?" he said. "Why the look? I think it's a fair exchange."

"I don't see the point," she said. "I don't have time for bullshit, Jack."

"It's not bullshit. No one knows what really happened nine years ago. Not even me, despite my best efforts. That's why I need your help."

That righteous glow was fading from Maddie's eyes. Now she just looked uncertain. Doubtful. Scared, even. He was losing her. *Damn.*

"I'll make it worth your while," he said hastily.

"I'll be so evil. Loathsome and slimy. A heartless seducer seeking only to devour. Elaine Moss's worst nightmare."

She laughed, to his relief. "Don't overdo it, or it won't be believable."

"They'd believe any terrible thing out of me," he said.

Maddie's laughter petered out. Damn. There were so many little buzzkills hidden between them. Emotional land mines, scattered around, blowing up in their faces when they least expected it. It made things so damn complicated.

"Would you take a look?" he asked. "I'm not trying to scam you, and I'm not asking you to come to conclusions that I like. There's no point in that. I just have a big pile of data, and I want you to take a look at it. I just want the truth."

"Jack, I'm absolutely the worst person you could ask," she told him. "The conflict of interest, my personal biases, they would corrupt everything I saw. You need to find someone impartial. Someone with no skin in the game."

"I've hired other people over the years," he told her. "They were useless."

"If they didn't find anything useful, then what makes you think that I will?"

"They're not as smart as you," he said simply.

"You're a Moss. You have a very strong ground-ing in science, and I think that will make the difference."

"I'm sure you could find someone well-grounded in science who isn't—"

"That's my condition. Take it or leave it. You do the math geek thing for me, and I'll do the comic book villain thing for you."

She let out a startled laugh. "You strike a hard bargain, Jack, but you've forgotten a small but important point. If by some wild chance, I should prove you innocent, then you would be instantly neutralized as a weapon to control Gran. It's your wicked scoundrel status that makes you uniquely useful to me. Talk about a conflict of interest."

He whistled under his breath. "Wow, Maddie. That's cold."

"Yes, it is," she agreed. "And I'm not sorry. I am thinking of myself first, for once in my god-damn life. Lucky you, to catch me on that spe-cial day."

Jack thought about it for a moment. "So we'll work on both projects simultaneously," he said. "I'll make an effort to scandalize your family while you study my data, but if you discover something to my advantage, I'll keep it a se-cret until Elaine lets you off the hook. Will you keep working on my project if Elaine stands her ground?"

"Of course. It's only fair. We should sit down somewhere. Talk terms."

"What kind of terms?" he asked.

She shrugged. "Ground rules. Parameters. Time frames. A general plan."

"Okay," he said. "Let's meet at the Seagull's Roost in Carruthers Cove tomorrow morning for breakfast, and hammer it all out. Nine o'clock?"

"Sounds good," she said.

They heard the quaver of an older woman's voice. A younger man's voice answering. Joanna Hollis emerged from the walkway out of the azaleas, clutching Aston's arm. Joanna spotted her, eyes lighting up. She dragged Aston in Maddie's direction.

Approaching from the other side was Gabe Morehead, his abs miraculously covered by a tux, holding a glass of champagne in each hand. Gabe sped up, in a clear effort to get to Maddie before Aston did.

"The vultures are circling," Maddie whispered. "Good Lord, deliver me."

"I could deliver you," he told her. "If you're absolutely sure you want me to."

"What do you mean?" she asked.

"Are you committed to this plan?"

"Of course. It was my idea in the first place. Hey!" She stiffened, as he pulled her against his chest. "What the hell are you doing?"

"Chasing away the vultures," he said, as he kissed her.

After the first breathless moment, Maddie found herself in a brand-new state of consciousness. One in which there existed nothing but the delicious sensation of Jack's hot mouth against hers, exploring, coaxing, persuading, seducing. Insisting.

Everything was irrelevant, and forgotten.

His taste was intoxicating. Her knees almost buckled as he flicked his tongue against hers. Her body reacted with a rush of helpless longing.

Maddie had imagined kissing Jack as a girl so many times, fantasizing in her bed, on those occasions that Caleb had brought him home for days at a time, parading him around in front of her hungry eyes. Gran and Grandpa Bertram both liked him so much, they'd been more than willing to open their home to him. Everyone loved Jack.

All those dream kisses added together did not begin to approach the reality.

A vague awareness of their spectators hovered on the edge of her consciousness. She could hear her rational mind in the distance, yapping ineffectually, but it couldn't drag her attention away from his delicious taste and scent, the heat, the dense, solid reality of him. His strong arms around her waist, her arms. Her arms, wound around his neck.

The kiss was getting more desperate. Her helpless, involuntary response was telling him dangerous, intimate secrets about herself, releasing feelings that had been buried under pressure for years. There was only this kiss, this man, this moment. Only his mouth, pleading, probing, plundering. His hands wound into her hair as their tongues stroked and danced and sucked. Her fingers dug in, trying to get a grip on the smooth fabric of his tux jacket. The stiff bulge of his erection against her belly made her want to get closer. To tie herself into knots with him. And pull them tight.

Slowly, she began to hear muffled giggles, slow clapping, amused murmuring.

Reality floated back. Consequences.

Jack lifted his head. His face was flushed, his eyes dazed. "Whoa," he whispered.

Maddie was gasping for breath. "What the hell just happened?"

"It was supposed to be a little bit of theater. It, uh…got away from me."

"We had an audience," she said.

"Wasn't that the point? Probably we were filmed. Somebody definitely whipped out their phone for a show like that. So I hope that you're sure about this."

"Yes, I am," she said, shakily.

They stared at each other, their eyes just inches apart. His parted lips were so sexy. That gorgeous mouth. His full, sexy lower lip. His dark eyes, boring into hers.

Theater. This is theater, Moss. Keep your head on straight.

"Jack," she whispered. "I never meant to imply that we'd…ah. You know."

"Of course not," he said swiftly. "I was just trying to make it convincing."

"Well, damn. You outdid yourself. Method acting. Couldn't be better."

Step back. Now. But her feet would not obey the command. That pull toward him came from deep inside. She couldn't control it.

"I think… I think I need to go to my room." Her voice shook.

"I'll walk you to your cabin," he said. "The whole place will be buzzing. And your grandma won't sleep tonight." He paused. "Neither will Caleb."

"He'll be fine," she said. "He has Tilda and Annika to console him."

"So? Shall I escort you?"

They paced in silence along the branching network of wooden walkways, lit by strands of fairy lights that glowed in the bushes and decorated the walkways. They passed several people, but Maddie avoided eye contact, ignoring smothered giggles and whispers.

They got to the narrow walkway that led off the main path, terminating at her own cabin, "The Lupin Lodge." She pulled her key card out of her evening bag.

"People are still watching," Jack said. "Let me come inside, just to put the cherry on top of our little fiction. I promise, I won't touch you in there. You can trust me."

She looked up at him, wishing it were true with an intensity that frightened her.

He looked so damn trustworthy. Sincere and passionate. She was so hungry for that. To be desired. Craved wholeheartedly. Desiring and craving in her turn.

She didn't want to resign herself to never finding that. To be bullied into settling for something less. This stolen moment with Jack reminded her of everything she stood to lose with Gran's stupid mandate.

The depth, the wildness, the realness, the magic. She craved it.

No, she craved him. Specifically. She craved Jack Daly. God help her.

And damn them all, for putting her back against the wall.

She beckoned him in. Jack stepped inside. Maddie closed the door, pulled the hanging blinds on the front window closed and flipped on the wall lamp by the bed. It cast a soft, rosy light. There were higher, brighter settings, but a few friendly shadows were just fine with her tonight.

"I hope I didn't offend you, back there on the terrace," he said. "I pulled a Bruce on you. It would've served me right if you'd smacked me. Or thrown a drink in my face."

She shook her head. "No, actually. That was the opposite of a Bruce. That guy's technique needs serious work. But he won't be practicing on me."

"So, you're saying that my technique is acceptable?"

"Yes," she murmured. "You were extremely convincing."

There was a brief, awkward pause.

"I should probably go," he said. "Whoever was watching us go inside has gotten bored by now. I'll see you tomorrow morning. At the restaurant."

"See you there," she echoed.

But their eyes stayed locked, and Jack hesitated by the door. "Sorry," he said. "It's hard to walk away. You look so beautiful in that dress."

"This? My bridesmaid dress?" She laughed out loud. "Oh, please. It's so poofy, and sea-foam green is not my color. But still. Thanks."

"It looks gorgeous on you. You look gorgeous in everything."

Maddie rolled her eyes, but smiled at him. "You're very kind."

Jack swallowed hard, and looked away. "Good night, then."

She didn't even know she intended to move, but suddenly she was at the door, blocking him. Her hand on the handle, holding it closed. "No," she blurted out.

Jack's eyes were wary. "No one's watching us now, Maddie."

Exactly. This was just for her. "Can you promise me something, Jack?" she asked.

"I don't make blind promises," Jack said slowly. "What is it that you want?"

"If I asked you to kiss me again, could you stop with just one kiss?"

His throat worked. "Yeah, I probably could," he said. "It would probably take years off my life, but, ah… I think I could do it."

"I will not have sex with you," she said. "That's a step too far, for me. A lot of steps too far."

"Understood," he said quickly. "Bad idea. The worst."

"But I'm in a selfish, dangerous mood tonight, and I really liked the way that kiss made me feel," she said. "I want to feel that way again."

"You're skating really close to the edge, Maddie," he said.

"I know. Just tell me, yes or no. Can you stop when I ask you to?"

"Ask yourself the same question," Jack said. "Don't put it all on me. I'm not the only one doing the kissing."

She swayed closer to him. "I am in no mood to analyze myself tonight. Are you going to kiss me, or are you going to get the hell out of my room?"

Jack made a rough sound deep in his throat, and seized her.

It was like before, but so much more. Wilder, hotter, deeper, now that they were alone in a locked room. The bed seemed to be exerting a magnetic pull, and they moved across the room toward it, kissing frantically all the way.

When the back of Jack's legs hit the bed, she gave him a little shove. He sat down abruptly at the foot of the bed. He stared up at her, panting.

Maddie kicked off her shoes and straddled him, hoisting up the billowing pale green skirt on either side of his legs, and settled herself against him, seeking the perfect angle where that bulge in the front of his pants was right where she needed it. Where she could rock against him, arms twined around his neck. Abandoning herself to that slow, sensual tongue-kissing that only he could do.

The straps of her dress had fallen down, showing the scalloped lace of her bra. Jack was cupping her breasts, peeling down the lacy fabric.

She leaned back, arching her back. Letting him look. His eyes on her body felt hot, deliberate, exciting. As palpable as a physical touch. She shivered at the sweet rush electrifying her skin, as his lips moved over her breast, and he drew her nipple into his hot mouth.

"God, Maddie," he muttered. "You're so beautiful."

Her voice was gone. Her fingers wound into his hair, her ragged breath catching with wordless whimpers at the tender swirl of his tongue... the deep, suckling pull...

This is Jack Daly. Pull this back. Before you hurt yourself.

But the answer that surged up from inside her was simple, and powerful.

No.

She felt lit up, from the inside. Shining like the moon, as he slid his hand under her skirt and between her legs. She moved against him helplessly, as he caressed her sensitive nub, then his hand slid deeper into her panties, exploring her fuzz of hair, the tender folds inside, the slick heat between them. He kept getting it just...exactly... right. Oh, God...

The pleasure that pulsed through her was so huge and startling, she almost fainted.

She collapsed, her head draped over his shoulder. Amazed, and abashed.

Jack nuzzled her throat, his hand still under her skirt, gently caressing her.

"Your skin is so soft," he whispered. "I love how you feel around my fingers when you come, squeezing me. You're so perfect."

She let out a jerky, helpless laugh. "Hardly."

Jack made a choked sound as she shifted against his erection. "Maddie," he said. "This is the end of my rope. I can't keep that promise any longer. If you don't want to have sex with me, then throw me out."

Oh, it was hard. But she lifted herself up and off him, reluctantly. Her face was very hot as she tucked her breasts back into her bra cups, and pulled up the straps of her dress. Her legs felt liquid in the aftermath of that orgasm. Her knees and ankles wobbled.

"I'm sorry if you feel used," she said.

"Oh, I don't," he said. "Don't worry about me. That was a peak life experience. I'll never be the same again." He backed slowly toward the door. "We still on for breakfast?"

"Why wouldn't we be?"

He pushed the door open. "Just wondering if this experience might have scared you off. But it looks like you're made of tougher stuff than that."

"I'm on a mission to emancipate myself, preferably without ruining my brothers' lives," she said. "A little sexual tension won't hold me back."

He stopped outside the door, and gave her a ghost of a smile. "A little?"

She laughed. "Okay, a lot of sexual tension."

"God help me. Good night, Maddie." The door swung shut.

Maddie sank down onto the floor, scared to death.

She'd couldn't believe herself. She'd done a dumb, dumb thing. She'd unleashed something that was too big and wild for her to wrangle. And she had no intention of walking it back. No intention at all.

Like she didn't have enough problems.

Five

Jack stared out the window of his cabin, at the little slice of ocean visible through the madrone trees. In the clear light of dawn, last night's pact with Maddie seemed even more rash and self-destructive than it had the night before.

He hadn't slept, partly from jetlag after flying from Johannesburg, but mostly from unsatisfied lust. Whether his eyes were open or closed, all he could see was Maddie Moss, straddling him, kissing him while he slid his fingers into her hot, slick, secret flesh.

Pleasuring her until she shattered in his arms.

Ah, great. There he went again, with the erection that just would not die, even when given a hand, quite literally. In the shower last night, and once again this morning, but he may as well have not bothered, for all the good it did.

The front desk had called him a taxi to take him down to the restaurant he'd suggested at Carruthers Cove. He got there in good time. The Seagull's Roost was busy at this hour, but he snagged a window booth with a sea view. He'd wanted a few minutes alone before she arrived, to get some practice in keeping his face composed.

He was in way over his head. No idea how to manage these feelings. He hadn't had this problem with Gabriella, or girlfriends before her. This was a brand-new problem. Frustration, grief, impotent rage...those were familiar. Routine, even.

But wild, frantic sexual desire...that was a whole other thing.

It was a long time since he'd felt frantic. To survive the BioSpark fallout, he'd buried his emotions very deep. It was the only way he could cope.

And all of his careful work had just gone straight to hell.

"Good morning."

Jack's heart bumped as he turned toward the source of the velvety feminine voice.

Maddie looked fresh and sporty, in a battered, silvery gray sweatshirt with a big colorful dragon stenciled on the chest and a pair of raggedy blue jeans that molded sexily to her gorgeous curves. Her hair was twisted up off her neck in a high messy bun, held in place by hair sticks that could double as lethal weapons if the need arose.

Her smile was brilliant, but she didn't sit down.

"Good morning to you," he replied. "Do I sense cold feet?"

"I just wondered if you might have them."

"Not me," he said. "You're the one with something to lose. I have no family left to alienate or scandalize, and no reputation left to trash. So why not?"

"I see your reasoning." She slid into the booth opposite him.

"But if you wanted to walk this back, I'd completely understand," he offered. "You'd have a hard time explaining that kiss on the terrace last night, but hey, you could always just blame it on me. I'll be your bad guy. I'm used to it."

Maddie folded her hands primly. "That's gallant of you, but I can take responsibility for my own indiscretions, thank you very much."

"Coffee, miss?" A white-haired waitress hovered near the table with the pot.

"Yes, please," Maddie said.

The woman filled her cup, topped up Jack's and left them with menus. They studied each other surreptitiously over the tops as they surveyed the day's specials.

"So how do we start?" he asked. "And where? Do you live in Seattle these days?"

"Yes, but I don't want to go home right now," she told him. "My family would get all up in my face. It would be impossible to concentrate."

"But don't you need to get back to work? Aren't you working at MossTech?"

"Not yet. Caleb wanted to make me official CFO, but with this marriage mandate nonsense, I figured it made no sense to take the job now. If I'm not married in two and a half months, Jerome fires us anyway, so why even start?"

"I see your point," he said. "So what are you doing in the meantime?"

"Not loafing," she said. "I took the opportunity to do some more consulting jobs in forensic accounting. I really enjoyed it."

"Gabe told me what you did for Darrell and Frederick's company."

Her eyebrows shot up. "Really? I'm surprised Gabe could even grasp what I did at Darrell and Frederick's."

"Ouch," he commented. "You are hard on your suitors."

"Only when they're clowning, half-dressed idiots," Maddie said. "Gabe Morehead is impossible to take seriously, even when his shirt is buttoned. What about you? What are you doing right now?"

"I'm working with a team in Johannesburg that's developing a new line of enzymatic recycling products," he said. "I've got meetings set up, the week after next. To discuss partnership possibilities for larger scale manufacturing."

Her eyes widened. "Oh. Wow."

"You look surprised," he said.

"I just didn't think—"

"That I would ever find work again in my field? It did seem that way for a while."

The waitress appeared to take their order, to his relief, breaking off this thorny line of inquiry just in time. Jack got a seafood omelet with home fries, and Maddie ordered French toast with a side of bacon.

"Back to us, and our strategy," Maddie said briskly, when the waitress had left. "As I said, I don't have an actual job right now, and I have nothing on my calendar that I can't postpone between now and Ava Maddox's wedding next weekend, so this week would be a great time to get started on both projects."

"Ava Maddox is getting married?" he said. "Wow. Her fiancé is a lucky guy."

"Yes, Ava's the best," Maddie agreed. "She's getting married to the Maddox Hill chief security officer, Zack Austin. They're madly in love. And my invitation has a plus-one. Would you go to the wedding as my fiancé? That'll drive Gran bananas."

The prospect made him uneasy. "Will Caleb and Marcus be there?"

"No," she assured him. "Marcus is in Southeast Asia, and Caleb is in Spain with Tilda, on the honeymoon that just won't quit. They're not supposed to be back for another ten days. Gran was invited, but I doubt that she'll go, since those things exhaust her. Besides, Annika is staying with her right now while her parents are traveling. It's a girls-gone-wild slumber party over there."

"I'll think about the wedding," he told her. "If you don't want to go back to Seattle yet, then why don't you come up to the Olympic Peninsula with me? I rented a house in the rainforest, right near Cleland. It's on the edge of a canyon, with rapids and waterfalls. You could get started there, if you don't want to be bothered by your family in town. Give me the time to rent myself a car, and you can just follow me right up to Cleland."

"Oh, I'll just drive you there," she told him. "Rent a car when you're up there. We just need to stop at a big stationery store to get some supplies, my whiteboards and markers that I'll need to live up to my end of the bargain. On the way up, we can start to chronicle a swoonworthy, torrid online romance. Maybe I'll get a big shiny ring, and we can make a great big deal about it on all of the socials—"

"I should be the one to get you the ring, right?"

"Wrong," she said sternly. "This is a theatrical production, and I'm the producer, so I fund the props. Duh."

"Okay, fine. Of course. Whatever."

"When it comes to lodging, though, I'm not sure if your mysterious secluded house hidden in the rainforest is quite the right choice for me," she said.

"No problem," he said swiftly. "There's a nice bed-and-breakfast in town just a couple miles away, run by the same woman who rents me the house. The last thing I want is to make you uncomfortable."

Her eyes slid away. "Um, yeah. About that. We have to address this…this thing between us."

"Our sexual attraction, you mean?"

"Well, yes. For lack of a better term."

"There is no better term," Jack said baldly. "That's literally what it is."

"Fine, fine. Call it what you will," she said, waving a dismissive hand. "So for all those many reasons we don't need to list right now, I'm stating, for the record, that giving in to that attraction would be a disaster. Isn't going to happen. Ever. Agreed?"

"Agreed," Jack said.

"We'll keep on exactly as we are right now," Maddie said. "I mean, look at us. We're just sitting here, like normal people, having breakfast. If we can do it here, we can keep on doing it. Right?"

"I won't come on to you," he assured her. "Except for those moments when we need to put on the show as an engaged couple. Like last night."

"Right." She bit her sexy lower lip. "Right. That's going to be…interesting."

"For lack of a better term," he said.

They both snickered under their breath.

Maddie savored a bite of her French toast. "I think it's doable," she said, as if trying to convince herself. "We just have to be really clear about the rules. For instance, can I call on you to keep this fiction going until it becomes irrelevant? Which is to say, my thirtieth birthday, or when Gran has a change of heart, whatever comes first."

"Of course. And for this entire period, you will keep an open mind and keep studying my data, until you feel like you've exhausted all possible avenues of inquiry."

"I can't guarantee that I'll find anything revelatory," she warned him. "In fact, I highly doubt that I will. But I do promise that I'll put my back into it."

"Thanks. That's all I want."

"But it's a very long shot," Maddie reminded him.

"So is your project," he said. "Knowing Elaine."

"Yeah, two lost causes. God knows why we bother."

"God knows," he echoed. "But let's have at it."

"Damn right," Maddie agreed. "So. The rules are, no kissing."

Jack laughed out loud. "That's out of character for us," he pointed out. "Aren't we supposed to be engaged? Isn't it supposed to be scandalous and juicy?"

"Fine, then. Kisses only when I say," she amended.

"Ah. Yeah. You mean, like last night in your room?"

Her face went rosy red. "Um, no. There will be no more of that nonsense," she said primly. "Chaste, controlled kisses. No crazy tongue action, or roving hands."

He couldn't stop grinning. "Okay, fine," he said. "Dry kissing on command. Frigid little pecks with tightly puckered lips."

"Don't you dare make fun of me. We have to keep a lid on this. When we get started, it's really hard to stop. So the only place to stop it is at the get-go."

"Of course," he assured her. "I'll be good."

The laughter had broken the tension. As they polished off their food and paid the tab, he realized that he was enjoying himself. Dangerous in itself.

Afterward, they strolled through the touristy town of Carruthers Cove, Washington, heading toward the parking lot where Maddie had left her car.

"Are you ready to take off for Cleland now?" she asked.

"My bags are still at the resort," he told her. "I checked out of the room, but I left my stuff in the luggage storage room and got a taxi down to Carruthers Cove this morning."

"Then I'll just drive you back up there to get your bags, and we'll take off."

Maddie dropped him off in front of the resort entrance. Bruce, Gabe and Aston were in the front lobby, and saw him getting out of Maddie's Mini Cooper.

They stared at him, open-mouthed, as he walked in and retrieved his bags.

"So it's true?" Bruce said slowly.

"Not sure what you're referring to," Jack said.

"I know girls like to go slumming, but I wouldn't have thought she'd stoop that low," Bruce said. "So, Maddie Moss is kinkier than I thought. That bad, bad girl."

Jack instantly weighed the pros and cons of putting his fist through Bruce's teeth, and just as quickly concluded that such a move would not help him achieve his goals.

Ice...cold...control. "Get out of my face, Bruce," he said.

"Hey there, fellas!" Maddie's voice was bright and cheerful. "Gorgeous morning, isn't it? I thought I'd come in and see if you needed any help with your bags, Jack."

"No, thanks. I'm good," he said, without breaking eye contact with Bruce.

Bruce's gaze dropped. Aston and Gabe exchanged knowing glances as he stomped away, muttering.

Maddie scooped up Jack's garment bag. "Shall we?" she asked briskly.

As they walked away, Maddie shot him a sidelong glance. "It looks like the hairy eyeball has begun," she murmured. "Our work here is done. Shall we hit the road?"

"Great idea." Jack tossed his stuff into Maddie's Mini Cooper, and got in.

As she pulled out onto the highway, he couldn't help feeling like he was escaping from some dark, cramped place and into freedom and possibility. Here he was, on a beautiful, coastal highway, in the company of a gorgeous woman who made his body tingle with sexual awareness. The windows were down, the air smelled sweet like rain and the sea. The side of the road was thick with brilliant golden poppies in the vivid green grass. Rainbows appeared in the mottled clouds without warning.

Maddie turned on the radio. A song played, about breaking down your walls.

Dad's voice in his head was kind, but stern.

Feet on the ground, Daly. You're cruising for a bruising, boy. Watch yourself.

Maybe so, but screw it. He couldn't get any more bruised than he already was, and he knew how to take it on the chin.

Hell, he'd gotten plenty of practice.

Six

After about twenty minutes on the coastal highway, Maddie saw the sign for Carruthers Bluff Road. She flipped on her turn signal.

"Where are we going?" Jack asked.

"We're taking a brief detour," she said. "There's something I want to see. When Caleb and Tilda got married, Gran confessed to buying us all a beach house out here, as a future wedding present. Can you believe it? Three beautiful beach houses, all in a row. Tilda and Caleb spent a few days here after their wedding, and loved it. But what with one thing and another, Marcus and I haven't even seen our future houses. Or rather, Gran's houses. They are hers, and hers they will probably remain, the way my life is going. But this might be a fun place to do some Instagram and Facebook stories that will make Gran froth at the mouth. I don't have the keys, but we can run around on the grounds."

"I'd rather not risk running into Caleb. Not until I have proof of my innocence."

They crested the top of the bluff, and a breathtaking view of the Washington beaches was visible in both directions. "Caleb isn't here," she reminded him. "He and Tilda are in Spain."

The sun was breaking through the clouds, a bolt of it hitting Paradise Point in the distance, the resort where they had spent the weekend. The sunlight lit up the green of the grass, the smudges of bright gold mixed into the green from the yellow poppies.

They came upon a row of mailboxes. "The first one is Caleb's," she said. "The next one is supposed to be mine. Shall we go and take a look?"

The driveway wound through green, flowering fields and trees. They passed Caleb's house, which she recognized from Tilda's photos and videos, and finally pulled up into a beautiful garden, exploding with multicolored flowers, outside a lovely old cottage.

It was sheltered by wind-twisted trees. Gray-shingled, time-weathered, exquisitely well-kept. Two stories, with a deep porch all the way around.

"Sweet," Jack said. "Elaine must have a really good gardener on call."

Maddie got out of the car, speechless. She walked over to the front porch, which was wide and beautiful, with plenty of room for porch furniture. There was a big swing facing the sea. She walked up the steps, peering through the windows into the rooms inside. They were lit up with sunshine, which showed all the gleaming hardwood planks, the paneling, the ancient beams in the ceiling. There were hanging baskets of blooming petunias and bleeding hearts at intervals on the porch.

Emotions she wasn't prepared for overflowed, and to her embarrassment, she found herself with tears running down her face.

"Wow," Jack said, startled. "What is it? Maddie? Are you okay?"

"Nothing, nothing. I'm so sorry." Maddie waved him away, digging in her pocket for a tissue. "It's this house. It just...pushes all of my buttons."

"Why? Don't you like it?"

"I love it," she said. "Of course, I love it. That's the problem. It's gorgeous. Everything about it is perfect. It's exactly what I like, and she knows it, because she knows me so well. And she's jerking me around with that, because she can. Like I'm a thing that belongs to her. She should trust me to live my life, not treat me like a baby."

Maddie lost it for a few minutes. When she lifted the tissue from her goopy face, Jack was standing a few feet away, looking uncertain.

"I'm sorry," he said. "I want to hug you. But that rule. It inhibits me. Are hugs permitted?"

She laughed, fishing for a fresh tissue. "Best not, I think." She blew her nose again. "You know what? I used to hate my mom for running away. But now, I totally get her. She might have been frivolous and selfish and shallow, but she was fighting for her life." She gave Jack a sideways look. "I expect you know the story of my mom, right?"

"Yeah. Caleb told me that she sent all of you kids off to your grandparents."

"She hadn't gotten around to sending me yet, but she would have soon enough," Maddie said. "She just wanted to party. She died when I was less than a year old. I used to be so angry at her for blowing us off like that, but she was just trying to breathe."

"What about your dad?" he asked. "Why didn't you go live with him?"

She shook her head. "Not an option," she said. "I don't even know who he is. No one did."

Jack looked pained. "Oh. I see. Not to judge, but maybe she could have found a way to breathe without abandoning her kids."

"Maybe," Maddie conceded. "Right now, I'm appreciating the advantages of extreme selfishness. She wasn't mired in guilt and responsibility, like me. And by all accounts, she certainly did enjoy herself."

"There has to be a balance," he said. "Between holding on to your principles, and maintaining your personal boundaries. Maybe that'll be the point of this whole experience for you. Learning where that sweet spot lies."

She laughed at him. "Jack Daly, life coach."

He shrugged. "Shitty things happen. What else can you do with that but try to find the lessons in them?"

"A wise observation," Maddie said. "Are you up for a little more theater?"

"Meaning what?"

"Meaning, I fix my mascara and lipstick, and you and I do a video shoot. I'm thinking, a romantic montage at the beach house of us exploring our future vacation home. We can go down to the private beach, and shoot some video of us frolicking in the surf, me jumping playfully up onto your back. Us walking away from the camera holding hands. Too bad I don't have a ring, but we can do another one later. I'll hashtag the crap out of it. #SheSaidYes, #HeProposed, #Beach-Fantasy, #WeAreEngaged, #HePoppedTheQuestion, #TyingTheKnot, #SurpriseEngagement, whatever else comes to me. Let's get this publicity machine humming."

"Sure, I'll do whatever. Pose me where you want me."

Maddie pictured Jack, stretched out on the bed, like last night. But this time, naked.

She turned away as heat rushed into her face. "I appreciate the helpful attitude," she said lightly. "So? Let's get started."

They wandered around the property, taking pictures, filming videos of each other, or of the two of them together. Blowing kisses at the camera, her laughing at him from under the hanging petunia baskets, making a heart shape with her hands. The two of them on the tire swing, each suspended upswing showing a stunning glimpse of the bluff, the ocean. The longer they went at it, the more silly, playful, romantic ideas came to them.

The time just slipped away, and finally Maddie looked down at her phone and was startled to realize that two and a half hours had gone by.

"We don't want to drive in the dark," she told him. "Let's wrap this up. A romantic kiss, with a beach view backdrop, and we'll call it good."

Jack's expression didn't change, but she felt the surge of heat in the air. Tension.

"On a scale of one to ten, how convincing do you want this kiss to be?" he asked.

She studied him, eyes narrowed. "Is that a trick question?"

"It's the opposite of a trick question. I'm trying not to step over the line."

"The kiss has to be hot," Maddie said. "Make it convincing. Make it a ten. If you can handle holding up the phone and kissing me at the same time."

He grinned at her. "I can walk and chew gum at the same time, Maddie."

"Yeah?" She handed him her phone. "Prove it."

Jack held it up. "Ready?"

"As I'll ever be."

Jack tapped the screen delicately with his fingertip, and leaned down.

Their lips touched, in a delicate, searching kiss. Then it softened, deepened into something that was suddenly bigger, and there they went again. Melting together, like always. The world fell away. She forgot everything she ever knew and just kissed him back, hungrily, with all the longing in her heart. She twined closer, heart thudding.

When Jack finally pulled away, they were silent. Sobered. Her phone lay forgotten in the grass, recording the empty sky.

Jack picked it up. "Damn," he muttered. "Sorry. I screwed that one up. Shall we try again? I'll prop it up on the porch railing this time."

"No," she said quickly. "No, we've got plenty to work with. Let's get going."

They got back onto the road. Maddie drove in self-conscious silence as Jack busied himself examining all the videos that they had shot.

"There's great stuff here," he told her. "I'm actually pretty good at editing videos. Want me to put together your romantic montages?"

"Sure, thanks. That would be great."

Pull it together, Moss. She had to dial this down. It was unmanageable. The tire swing, the heart hands, the kiss.

Already, she was wishing it was real.

Seven

The only way to survive was by keeping busy.

Jack had learned this life-saving trick even before BioSpark. He'd learned it after Dad died, living in that string of foster homes. If he kept his mind fully occupied, he could keep moving forward somehow, like riding a bike. That was one of the reasons he'd hit the books so hard at school. Savage focus on studying had been his only refuge.

So to that end, he opened up the back of the car when they stopped for lunch on the road, and pulled his laptop out of its carrying case.

Jack downloaded the video clips they had shot, once they had ordered lunch, and got to work with all the focus of a guy expertly sublimating his sexual energy into another activity. His fingers chattered on the keys as he manipulated the tiny videos, trimming them, timing them. In not too long, he'd come up with three short video montages.

Maddie watched, fascinated, as she sipped her iced tea through a straw. "You're so smooth with that program," she said. "Where did you learn to do that?"

Jack didn't even break stride. "After I got out of jail, I was flat-ass broke," he said. "I used up all my money for my legal defense. Some friends believed in me, but I didn't want to lean on them. And I couldn't get work in my field, for years. So I did a bunch of random jobs. I worked on a fishing boat in Alaska for a while. Stank of fish for months afterward. I worked construction jobs, I tended bar, I worked for a PR company, creating content for social media accounts. I got pretty fast at this kind of stuff."

"Did you ever find work that you liked more than what you did before?"

He gave her a level look. "No."

Maddie winced. "Sorry. I shouldn't have asked that."

"It's okay. Hey, if you want these videos to pop,

we need a few clips of music. I'm thinking, blues, rock, steel guitar. Something gritty and rebellious, with a heavy beat."

Maddie's golden eyes widened, and she smiled. "Oh yeah. I know just the song." She lifted up her phone and selected it from her playlist, offering him her earbuds.

He put them into his ears, and listened to the first few bars. "Wait, isn't this the group that did that song that played for Trix and Terrence's first dance?"

"Yes, it is," she replied. "Moon Cat and the Kinky Ladies. It's my little niece's favorite band. This is their latest single. Listen to the words. A single verse should be about the right length, and there are three verses, one for each video."

Jack raised the volume and listened to the girl singer's wispy, and yet somehow compelling voice.

You say my skirt's too short,
My lips as red as fire,
Now you're calling all my shots,
But you're making me a liar,
I know you want to say,
It's just my restless heart to blame,
But I just can't wear,

Oh, I just can't wear,
No, I just can't wear,
Your golden chains.

"That's perfect," Jack said. "And exactly fifty seconds, too." Jack deftly applied the three clips of the song to accompany the videos, and then spun the laptop around so she could see the result.

Just as the first video ended, the waitress brought their sandwiches. Grilled cheese on sourdough for her, corned beef on rye for him, tomato basil soup for both of them.

Maddie set the second video to play again as she took a bite of her sandwich.

"They're perfect," she told him, after she'd watched them all twice. "Like those advertisements for high-end luxury products, for cars, jewelry, perfume. Where you can't quite figure out exactly what they're advertising, but you still want some."

"That's the vibe I was going for," he told her.

"Can I go ahead and post them?"

"Sure, be my guest. Let me just send you the final files."

In a few moments, Maddie had uploaded the first video, and was holding her finger over the post button. "Here goes," she said. "Fully braced for family disapproval."

"I'm glad you have a family to disapprove," he said.

Her smile faded "Oh. I'm sorry I—"

"No, no. I didn't mean to lay guilt on you. I mean it literally. I lost my dad when I was fourteen, but he would've liked you. He would've been sorry this wasn't real."

Just like me. He pushed the thought back down into the depths. Not now.

Maddie posted the video, and snapped her laptop closed. "I'm sorry you lost him."

"Me, too, but that was the one thing I was grateful for, when everything went to hell," Jack said. "Dad never had to see me in handcuffs or shackles. A prison jumpsuit."

"I'm so sorry," Maddie said again.

"It's one of the reasons I need to clear my name," he went on. "It's for him, even though he's gone."

Jack saw her smile fade, and stopped talking. She didn't believe him, and after the fun and laughter all afternoon, that realization was jarring.

She might never believe him. He just had to swallow that down and behave like a gentleman, because that's just what you did. Dad would've wanted it.

There's no excuse not to be classy, son. Not in any situation.

Maddie's phone began to ring as Jack paid the tab. She looked at the display, and glanced at him, eyes sparkling. "Word is spreading," she said, holding her smartphone up. The display read "Gran." "Our work has been seen and evaluated."

The phone kept buzzing. "Are you going to answer her?" he asked.

Maddie shook her head. "Too soon. First, I let her sweat." She declined the call and typed in a text message, holding it up for him to read.

I'm fine. Don't worry. Just trying to do my duty to family and MossTech. I'll contact you when I get back into town.

"What do you think?" she asked. "Too snarky?"

He whistled as he read it. "Oh, man. That's gonna sting."

"Yep, that's the whole point," she said with grim satisfaction, tapping the screen. "There, it's sent, and the phone is off. I am officially incommunicado."

"You just can't wear those golden chains."

"Exactly," Maddie said.

When they were in the parking lot, she pointed toward the strip mall they had driven through. "I saw a big stationery store a mile or so back," she said. "Let's stop there and pick up my whiteboards and markers."

"Whatever you need," he said. "I wasn't expecting you to hop right to it."

"You came through for my project, so it's only fair. And the videos are a great beginning. I feel better now that I'm doing something proactive, other than just scrambling for eligible bachelors, feeling all sweaty and desperate and uptight. It's so not me, you know? It feels good to just be my own wacky self."

"I'm happy to help your wacky self," he informed her. "I'm also glad that my trashed reputation is actually good for something, for once."

After a quick stop at the stationery store, they packed the supplies into the car and got back on the road, Jack driving.

The afternoon on the bluff, the video and lunch had drained away the tension between them. They still had to steer around the danger zones, but they were getting used to them, and there was still plenty left to talk about. With a little judicial prodding, he got her to tell him all about the twists and turns of her career path. How she discovered the thrills of forensic accounting entirely by accident, while getting her MBA. She'd been interning at a hedge fund in New York, and one of the senior partners had been cooking the books.

She had been the one to find the breadcrumbs, and trace them back to the source. To piece it all together.

"And that's what you'd prefer? More than being CFO for MossTech?" he asked.

She nodded. "Yeah, I'm not really the type to be an executive. Caleb's better at that kind of thing than me. I like getting into the weeds, really going deep, and I don't think executives ever have a chance to do that. They're too busy dealing with the big picture. I've studied forensic accounting in all different kinds of industries, and I've even developed some of the latest technological tools for it myself. Although nothing will ever replace my precious whiteboards. But I use it all, simultaneously."

"You actually make it sound interesting," he said. "I can hardly believe it."

That made her laugh, which felt like a conquest. He loved the curve of her luscious lips, the way her dewy brown skin glowed. Her bold cheekbones. Her bone structure was elegant, striking. Regal, even. Every now and then, he caught a glimpse that made him think of Caleb, but not much. She must take after her father. And the guy must've been damn good-looking, to generate a gorgeous creature like her.

"What?" she demanded. "Watch the road, Daly."

"You don't look much like Caleb, or Marcus," Jack said. "I've seen pictures of your mother, and Caleb looks a lot like her. But you don't. Do you have any pictures of your dad?"

"I've got nothing," she said. "Not a name, not even a nationality. My mother never got around to discussing my parentage with anyone. The only thing the housekeeper was pretty sure about was that my father was not her current boyfriend, the guy with the yacht. Yacht guy was a redhead. Definitely not my progenitor."

"No, I would say not," he agreed.

"We did a genetic test once, a few years ago, out of curiosity," she told him. "The Moss side is English and Irish. Caleb has Spanish and Portuguese ancestry, Marcus has Japanese and some Korean, and mine is mainly Ethiopian and Egyptian, and some other countries in Africa. We're a global grab bag. My mother had wide-ranging tastes."

"The results were pretty damn optimal. You're all extremely good-looking."

"Thanks. The housekeeper thought that my father might have been a musician who was in town on tour, but she didn't know his name, or even what instrument he played," Maddie said. "My mother never wore any golden chains. She just left me with the housekeeper and partied like a maniac. Up to the very end."

"I'm sorry about the accident, but I'm glad you weren't on that yacht," Jack said.

"Me, too. I'm grateful for my grandparents and my brothers, however much I bitch. I know I've been blessed. I try not to complain, but lately, it's got the better of me."

"You have a right to feel how you feel," he assured her. "It's better to just unload it. You breathe easier when you aren't trying to be perfect."

There was a silence, and they both broke into smothered, startled laughter.

"I promise I won't try too hard," she told him. "What about your mom? I knew about you losing your dad when you were fourteen, but I never heard about your mom."

"Cancer," he said. "She died when I was six."

Maddie winced. "Ouch. Jack. I'm so sorry."

"Thanks," he said. "It was a long time ago, but it was harrowing. I remember her, but just barely. Like a warm glow through a curtain. I wish I could remember specifics, but Dad's gone, too, so there's no one who can help me with the details. Time just grinds them all away."

"You're still lucky," Maddie said. "I can't remember my mother at all. Not even a glow. You must have pictures, right? Do you look like her? Or your dad?"

"My complexion is hers, dark hair and eyes, but everything else is my dad."

"Did you get those long eyelashes from her?"

He laughed. "Must have. Hard to say."

The miles sped by. Their conversation wound on, long and meandering. They talked about anything and everything, and by twilight, he was making his way through Cleland, the town nearest to his vacation house.

"My suggestion is, we check you into your B and B, and then go to the Broderick Tavern for dinner, since it's right nearby," he said. "I'll show you the house, and we'll put up your whiteboards in a spare bedroom. Then you can head off to your B and B whenever you're ready."

"Sounds great," she said. "It's so beautiful here."

"Yeah, I always stay up here, since I discovered this town, and this house. The forest relaxes me. I could take you on some of my favorite hikes, if you're into that kind of thing. I love big mysterious forests. They put my problems into perspective."

"I'd love it," she said. "I adore hiking. And forests. I want my problems put into perspective, too. It sounds very therapeutic."

Jack pulled over in front of the large, brightly painted Victorian house that belonged to Delilah, the woman who rented him the vacation house. Delilah came out to greet him, rattling a bunch of keys. She had a cloud of curly silver hair and was dressed in a brilliant tie-dyed T-shirt. "Jackie!" she sang out. "Glad you're back, handsome. The house is all ready for you. I even picked up some of those cinnamon rolls you like from the bakery and left them on the counter."

"Thanks, Delilah. Hey, could you rent my friend a room in your B and B?"

Delilah looked distressed. "Oh, honey, I'm so sorry to disappoint you, but we have a fiftieth wedding anniversary in town, and they all checked in today. I'm full to the gills. If you'd asked me two days ago you could've had any room you liked."

"Yikes." He shot Maddie a worried glance. "I figured, since it was a Monday evening..."

"That's almost always true, just not today," Delilah said regretfully. "I'd send her to the Eagles Nest, but Kris is full up, with two weddings. Your best bet is the Marriott in Beckinsdale."

"It's a half-hour drive back the way we came," Jack said.

"I know, hon. So sorry. If all else fails, there are plenty of extra full-size sheets for the other bedrooms. I just made up the bed in the master bedroom."

"Okay. Thanks." Jack turned to Maddie. "I'm so sorry."

"It's fine," she assured him. "It's a straight shot back to Beckinsdale. I think I saw the Marriott near the south freeway entrance, right?"

"Yes, that's exactly right." Delilah's curious blue eyes darted between her and Jack. "Shall I call and make a reservation for you?"

Maddie smiled. "Thanks, but I'll handle it."

Jack waited outside while Maddie found the Beckinsdale Marriott on her phone, and booked herself a room. When she hung up, she strolled alongside him toward the Broderick Tavern while scanning her text messages.

"Gran texted eight times," she said. "Caleb, four times. Tilda, three. Marcus, three. Even Annika called me. They're out of their freaking minds."

"Are you going to read the messages?"

"Maybe later. Right now, I'm channeling Susanna Moss and thinking of only myself. Let's see how our video montage is doing out in the world." She clicked it, and looked up, eyes sparkling. "It's been viewed nine hundred times so far."

"That's wild. But good, for your purposes. Right?"

"Right," she said. "Very good."

"Any regrets?" he asked.

Her eyes flashed at the challenge. "Hell, no."

"Ahh." Jack held open the door to the Broderick Tavern. "That's my girl."

Eight

Maddie savored a bite of her grilled marinated halibut, and pulled out her notebook. The food was great, the ambience was relaxing, there was even live music playing in the back of the room, and it wasn't half bad. She was having way too much fun.

It was unfortunate, that the B and B had no rooms, but whatever. It just meant that she had to drive, and therefore couldn't drink with dinner. Just as well, considering. With Jack, she certainly didn't need any help lowering her inhibitions.

She pulled out her black-rimmed geek-girl glasses and put them on. "Okay, Jack. Behold me in work mode. Let's get started."

"They look great," he said. "The $E=mc^2$ vibe is very hot. Works for me."

"So glad you like it," she said. "So. What I want from you now is an overview of what I have to analyze. I also want to know who looked at the records before, and why you felt that their efforts fell short. And if you have their documentation, great."

"I have it all in my files," he said. "I'll show it to you back at the house. But it's been a long day. Wouldn't you rather get started tomorrow?"

"Gran always says, why put off till tomorrow what you can do today? Gimme the goods."

"I see why you Mosses are freakish overachievers," Jack said ruefully.

"Yeah, we're twisted that way. So? What can you tell me?"

Jack got a look on his face that she'd noticed before. Like he was bracing himself.

"You know about the products we were developing at BioSpark, right?"

"I have a rough idea, but it was a long time ago," she said. "Also, I was off in college at the time, and Caleb doesn't talk about it. So refresh my memory."

"We called them the Carbon Clean line. The base was a cocktail of selected bacteria and fungi that produced super-enzymes that could digest plastic. We had a range of products. Some for landfills, others for water. Time release capsules for oceans, lakes and rivers."

"That much I do remember," she said. "There was lots of buzz. I remember the adulation. Magazine covers, interviews, screaming fangirls, like you two were rock stars. It went straight to Caleb's head. He thought he was God's gift back then, though he had his hands full with Tilda. How about you? Were you involved with anyone?"

Maddie knew the answer to that question perfectly well, having consumed every last scrap of news ever published about Jack Daly. But he never needed to know that.

"I was with Gabriella Adriani back then," Jack told her. "Our head of marketing."

"Oh, yeah. I remember her. Super thin, platinum blonde, very black eyebrows?"

"That's her. Caleb and I were too busy to be distracted by screaming fangirls."

"Right. So, BioSpark made the Carbon Clean line, and everyone was really excited about it. Who dreamed that up, anyhow? Caleb never told me."

"I guess it was me, at the beginning," Jack

said. "One of my summer jobs when I was at Stanford was at a dump and recycling center. I spent hot summer days in a festering trash heap. Man, was it ripe."

"I just bet it was," she said.

"I noticed that in some places, the plastic was degrading faster than in others. So I took samples from the slime, and cultured them. My coworkers at the dump thought that I had psychological problems, rooting around in the stinking trash. They called me the Garbage Guy."

"Inspired," Maddie said.

"Anyhow, Caleb and I selected the microbiomes that were the hungriest, looking for the super-enzymes. When we found them, we modified the genes to supercharge the process. It took years of iterations to find a balance of microbes that would make degrading plastic economically viable."

"Hence, your preoccupation with balance."

"Maybe. Anyhow, that was the first version of Carbon Clean. We recruited a dream team of our favorite researchers, microbiologists, organic chemists and geneticists. We fine-tuned it into something that worked. And I mean, really worked. We were about to go public. And the sky fell."

Jack looked away, his throat moving.

Maddie helped him out. "Energen Corp came out with almost the same product."

"So you do remember," he said.

"The broad strokes, yes. The news was full of it. Caleb was...well, never mind."

"I know how he felt." Jack's voice was bleak. "Someone set me up."

And there they were again, at the heart of her dilemma. How could she proceed in good faith if she didn't believe his story? Maddie tapped her pencil against her notebook.

"So tell me, Jack," she persisted. "How am I supposed to help you?"

"Whoever did this plotted for a long time," Jack said. "It wasn't an impulse. And Energen could never have come up with a product like ours out of nowhere. It took us years, with top-notch researchers and a sizable budget. And we were busting our asses, working like mani-acs, never sleeping. As far as the Energen team goes...well, Joel LeBlanc, their lead guy? He was no heavyweight, and that's putting it kindly. He was a mediocre biochemist no one had ever heard of, and no one on his small team had ever stuck out in the crowd, either. And yet, with a fraction of the time, resources and personnel, they pulled a product very similar to ours out of their asses. Ta-da. Energen Vortex was presented to the world."

"And Caleb knew this about them?"

"At that point, Caleb was no longer listening to me," Jack said. "Someone planted all that evidence on me. He couldn't get past that, and I don't blame him. It looked bad."

"Refresh my memory," Maddie said. "What was the evidence?"

He let out a slow breath. "A couple days before the Energen public offering, a broker filled an order to buy seven hundred thousand dollars of Energen stock," he said. "But the broker came forward afterward, and said that the request came from my IP address. My desktop computer at home. As if I would be stupid enough not to mask my IP, if it were me who placed the order."

"You couldn't have been hacked, or spoofed?"

He reluctantly shook his head. "Not with the kind of encryption we had in place. It was made to order, exclusive, specific to us. The order was placed a little after two in the morning. They also found bank accounts in Panama that I had ostensibly set up, and a plane ticket to Rio that I never bought. The whole scene was meticulously organized."

"You were in the apartment alone when this order was placed?"

"I was asleep," he said flatly. "I'd drunk a glass of wine with Gabriella, and crashed."

"How much was the Energen stock worth, after the company went public?"

"About forty-six million dollars," he said. "Confiscated, of course. Not that I would have kept it in any case."

Maddie was relieved that the details he cited matched up with her own version of events...so far. "That's quite a chunk of money," she mused. "But it's very small change for Energen, particularly now. Energen's Vortex product must've earned billions by now."

"It has." Jack's voice was bitter. "And their product is weaker than ours. It's slower, less reliable, it has problems in salt water, it has problems at both lower and higher temperature ranges, it's useless on polystyrene and polyvinyl chloride... they're hacks. They stole a perfectly functional thing, and covered their tracks by fucking it up."

Maddie studied his face. He was so believable. Then again, Caleb had been taken, too, and Caleb was no fool. "Tell me something, Jack," she said.

"Anything," he said.

"If you're so sure that Energen stole BioSpark's research, why not accuse them and nail them to the wall?"

Jack hesitated. "I'm not supposed to have some of this information, about Energen's research and development timeline."

"Meaning what? You have it or you don't."

"Not exactly," Jack said. "I have a friend who shared inside info with me. But she still works there, and if they knew she told me, she'd be shredded by their legal department. Her career would be over, if she didn't end up in jail. So I can't show this stuff to the police. Besides, it's inconclusive. It paints a picture, it suggests things, it points. But there's no smoking gun in the mix."

"So you have information that's useless," Maddie said ruthlessly. "You can't use it without exposing your friend. So why should I take it seriously? Why should anyone? And what's the point, if you can't clear your name?"

"I just want to prove to my best friend that I never sold him out," Jack said forcefully. "I squeezed my source because I hoped the data would at least point me in the direction of the person who wanted to destroy me. So that I can tear him to pieces."

Maddie's spine stiffened. "I want no part of any violence."

"No, no," Jack assured her. "Metaphorically speaking."

Maddie tapped her pen frantically against the notebook, pondering that. "Who's your source?" she asked. "Can you even tell me?"

"Will you promise to keep it to yourself?"

Maddie gave him a narrow look. "You're asking for a big leap of faith."

"Please, Maddie. I need your word. I don't want to hurt my friend."

She hesitated for just a moment. "Okay, you have my word. But I don't see the point, if you can't use the data. It's not like you can get that money back."

"It was never about money," Jack said. "Money was just a byproduct of what we were doing. It's useful, for moving forward, but it doesn't drive me. It never has."

Maddie nodded. "Fine. I get it. Tell me about your secret source."

"Her name is Amelia Howard, and she works in the R & D department of Energen. She's an administrator, not a researcher."

"And I'll be looking at her data tomorrow?"

"Among other things," Jack said. "Gabriella introduced us. Amelia rented a condo in our complex. I had an apartment down in San Francisco, but I came up to Seattle so often, I decided to keep an apartment here, too, and Amelia and I became friends. She's a sweet person. She was breaking up with a real turd of a guy who treated her like dirt, and I was trying to be supportive of her. Then my world fell apart. We were both a mess."

"I need to talk to Amelia," she said. "I agree to not expose her role in sharing data with you, but I still want to look her in the eye and ask her all my questions."

Jack nodded, and pulled out his phone, selecting a number. "I'll see if she'll talk to you," he said, as it rang. "Hey, Amelia?... Yeah, it's Jack. I'm back in town... Yeah, staying up in Cleland again. Yeah, I'd love to. Let's set something up. Hey, I've got a favor to ask of you. I've asked a friend of mine to analyze my BioSpark archives... Yeah, I know... Uh-huh. She was hoping to talk in person... No, she's given me her word... Hold on and I'll ask." He looked at Maddie. "When could you meet her? This week, next week?"

"How about after Ava's wedding next weekend?" Maddie said. "I could meet her on Sunday, if she prefers not to do it on a weekday. We could grab lunch. Someplace discreet, where no one will see me with her."

Jack relayed all of this, and then closed the call, slipping the phone in his pocket. "Twelve-thirty on Sunday," he confirmed. "She sent me the address of a bistro near her place where you two can get lunch. I forwarded it to you."

"Great. I look forward to talking to her. So? Anything else?"

"That's my backdrop," Jack said. "The broker told everyone about the order I was supposed to have made, but didn't. BioSpark's public offering tanked. I was arrested, for fraud, malfeasance, insider trading. And I went to prison."

"But you got out after six months," Maddie said. "How did you manage that?"

"Random luck," he said grimly. "The crime scene was poorly handled. There were mistakes made by the criminologists, so some of the key evidence was inadmissible. So it was enough to convince everyone that I was guilty, but not enough to convict me, at least not for very long. All I want now is to be able to convince Caleb that it wasn't me."

Jack sounded so sincere. She was almost tempted to entertain the possibility that he really was innocent. But that was dangerous. She liked that story. Liked it way too much.

The waitress came back. "Dessert? Another drink? Coffee?" she asked them.

"I'm fine," Maddie said. "We should call it a night, after I get you home."

"I hate to have you drive all the way back to Beckinsdale," Jack said.

"Oh, I'll be fine. I'll drop you at your house and head on out. I want to get started bright and early tomorrow."

The winding road through the forest was eerie in the headlights of her car. Even in the dark, she was charmed by the house when they arrived. It was a bold modern design, interlocking steel-and-glass cubes that let all light and the colors of the forest in. It was perched on the edge of a narrow canyon. One of the terraces cantilevered out over the canyon, right over the rushing rapids and waterfalls. The scent and sound of the place was a sensory embrace, a great chittering and humming, chirping of birds and insects, the rustle of wind in the branches, the sweet, cool smell, the constant rush of water.

The inside of the glass house was understated and comfortable. Soft couches in warm earthy colors were grouped around the stone fireplace.

There was a big, welcoming kitchen, and a long wooden table, big enough to seat twelve.

"Hey," he said. "I just thought of something. Why don't you stay here, and I'll just drive to Beckinsdale? The bed's made up, the bathroom's ready. Just settle in and relax."

"No way," she said. "This is your place."

"But I don't want you to—"

"You know what?" she said, on impulse. "I won't go to Beckinsdale. I'll crash here. I just decided. It's silly for me to drive all that way when you have plenty of room." She paused. "Unless you're uncomfortable with that, of course," she added.

"Of course not." Jack looked pleased. "That would be great. I'll go and find those sheets and fix up your bed right away."

"Let's get those whiteboards set up tonight, so I can start at first light."

"Will do," Jack called from one of the bedrooms.

Maddie turned on the phone to call the hotel to cancel the reservation, and saw messages piling up. Missed calls from everyone in her family, and some of her friends. Geri alone had called three times. There were dozens of text messages. Word was out.

The phone began to buzz. This time it was Caleb. *Not tonight, bro. Not a chance.*

She declined that call, and went into the family group chat.

For God's sake, people, relax. I'm fine. I'll get in touch when it suits me. Give Annika a kiss for me. Later, people.

Take that, Gran. Attitude to the utmost.

Nine

Jack woke up from a restless doze, and smelled coffee and toast. It was barely light. He looked around, disoriented, until the events of the last few days suddenly hit his conscious mind, knocking him right back down onto his back. Freshly astonished.

He stared up at the ceiling in disbelief. Maddie Moss, in all her seductive gorgeous glory, was in the other room, studying his BioSpark archives. Miracles did exist.

Of course, she was biased against him, but hey, she was here, and that was huge. He had to keep his cool. Stay the hell out of her way. Try not to stare, if at all possible.

He washed his face, brushed his teeth, threw on some sweatpants and a T-shirt, then grabbed a cup of coffee from the kitchen, noticing toast crumbs on a butter knife in the sink. The rooms were all on one side of the corridor, and a wall of glass was on the other, showing the forest in the misty dawn.

He pushed open the spare bedroom door they had prepared last night. Maddie stood with her back to him, staring at one of her whiteboards, a black marker in one hand and a piece of toast in the other. The table behind her held her laptop, markers, piles of Post-it notes. Her notebooks.

"Good morning," he said.

"Morning." Her voice was faraway. "Can't talk. Gimme a sec."

"Sure, sure. Carry on," he said.

A few minutes later, she joined him in the kitchen and refilled her coffee cup. "I didn't mean to be rude, but I was chasing a thought," she said.

"Sorry to interrupt you," he said. "Did you catch it?"

"I hope so. Time will tell."

She wore the same baggy sweatshirt she'd had on at the beach bonfire party, but today she wore soft striped athletic leggings instead of cutoff blue jeans. It was a mystery how slouchy athletic wear could be so sexy on her. Her hair was tied up off her face with a scarf, with an explosive twist of ringlets showing on top. She wasn't wearing makeup. Her unpainted lips were a deep blush rose. The skin on her face was so exquisitely supple and soft. He'd memorized every detail from that last kiss. His fingers ached to feel it again.

"You know, Jack, I've been looking through stuff, and this thing really is not my area of expertise," she admitted. "I'm a hard numbers kind of woman. This involves comparing BioSpark's research to Energen's, right down the line. A whole other thing."

He was crestfallen. "So you don't want to continue?"

"I never said that. Truthfully? I'm hooked. I really want to see more. It's just that it makes me less confident of being absolutely sure of my results."

Something inside him relaxed. "That's fine," he said. "I'm just happy to have a smart person with fresh eyes looking at the whole mess again. That's all I need. I don't need guarantees or certainties. I already know that I can't have them."

"But it will take a while," she warned him. "I

like to lay out everything where I can see it, and then organize it, and reorganize it. For a while, it's like waiting for popcorn to start popping. Right when you start to wonder if the kernels are all duds, it starts to happen all at once. Ideas and patterns start bubbling up."

"Should I stay out of your way?"

"For the most part. I tend to be kind of rude when I'm concentrating. But I'd like to have you within shouting distance, in case I need elucidations about microbiomes, or super-enzymes, or bioremediation, or breaking polymer links, or what all."

"Fine. I just need to run in to town to grab some groceries. Can I use your car?"

"Of course. Feel free." Her eyes were already far away, and she was tapping her pen against that little notebook. "The keys are in my purse."

He forced himself to drag his eyes away from the spectacular back view of Maddie Moss, which he could gaze at worshipfully forever. So hot, working at her whiteboards, standing on her tiptoes, reaching above her head, which lifted up the sweatshirt and showed off the shape of her butt, and the pink, narrow bottoms of her highly arched feet.

He drove to the farmers' market, the grocery

store, the bakery. When he got back and hauled in all the bags, Maddie had moved on to another whiteboard.

Some of the info she was noting down was familiar, but the way she organized her information was not comprehensible to him. It looked almost sloppy, but clearly, it wasn't, judging from the laser focus in her eyes, and the way she utterly ignored him. If he weren't so invested in her conclusions, he might even get his feelings hurt. As it was, no.

You go, girl. Do your thing. Don't ever stop.

He came in a couple of hours later, and found her seated at the computer, tapping away. Yet another whiteboard was full of scribbling, which he studied, fascinated. "Could you tell me what you're doing?"

"No," she said, without looking at him.

"Ah. Okay. I'll make us some lunch. Gotta fuel the magic machine."

Maddie didn't even change expression. "Huh?"

He left her to it with a snort, and went to fire up the grill. Then he wrapped a salmon fillet in foil, loaded it with butter, lemon and dill. When the meal was organized on the terrace, along with some fire roasted summer vegetables and some fluffy rice pilaf, he opened the door. "Hey, I've got food," he told her. "Out on the terrace."

She turned to him, her eyes blank. He could almost hear the gears grinding loudly in her head as she dragged her mind back to a plane where such things as food existed.

"Thanks," she said, distractedly. "Uh...yeah. Be right there."

"We'll eat outside," he said. "Come whenever you're ready."

She looked down at her hands, which were blackened with ink from the markers. "I'll just go and wash up."

Maddie was quiet as they were eating, but he didn't take it personally. He remembered that zone, from college, from grad school, from Bio-Spark. She'd forgotten how to talk, and it took a while to remember. The deeper you went, the harder it was to come back.

"By the way, when I was shopping in town, I saw a jewelry store," he said. "If you want, we can go there, and make another video that's all about the ring."

"Oh, yeah. I'm glad you reminded me," she said. "I'd forgotten all about that. It's important to feed the beast."

"Have you checked in with your folks?"

"You mean, have I glanced at their hysterical text messages? Not since last night. Let's see the heights of madness they've risen to now."

Maddie pulled out her phone and turned it on, and it immediately began to ring.

"It's Tilda," Maddie said, studying the display. "I love her like a sister, but not now. Their timing is insane. Every time I turn on my phone, it rings instantly. I can't face it."

"What time did you wake up?"

"I was already working at 4 a.m.," she said. "I didn't sleep well."

"No? Was the bed okay?"

"The bed was fabulous. I love those trees, and the sound of the water. But I was restless, so I got up and went to work." She clicked through messages, and gasped in dismay. "Oh, God."

"What is it? Is everyone okay?"

She clapped her hand over her eyes. "Caleb is cutting his and Tilda's Spain trip short. They're flying home from Barcelona today. To deal with me."

"Yikes," he said. "That's awful."

"Yes, it really is."

"At least your gran is okay," he said. "You scared me for a second."

"You thought I'd given her a stroke or a heart attack? No way. She's a tough old bird."

Jack just shrugged and looked away.

Maddie leaned over the table and tapped his arm. "Hey. What's wrong? Are you upset about something?"

"I just wish that we were messing with people I dislike," he said. "Like Bruce Traynor, for instance. Jerking him around would be a blast. But it's no fun doing it to people that I care about and respect, like Caleb and Elaine."

Maddie stared down at her food. "Dammit, Jack. Stop. You're making me feel guilty, and that's exactly what I'm trying to avoid right now."

"Sorry," he said sheepishly. "I'll shut up and get you some pie."

"Great. Then we go ring shopping, and I can compound my cruelty to my family even more. Ruthless, monstrous hag that I am."

Jack cut her a slice of blackberry pie with shortbread crust, and scooped up a sphere of honey vanilla ice cream. "As you command, Oh Dreadful One," he said. "Your evil truly knows no bounds."

"I'm sure that's exactly what Caleb is saying about me to Tilda right now in the airport at Barcelona," Maddie said. She took a bite of pie and gasped with pleasure. "Oh, my God, Jack. This is freaking divine."

Yes. So far, so good. He was keeping it classy.

After lunch, they went to the jewelry store. The town was a tourist haven for wealthy Seattle residents, so there was a large selection of beautiful, unique designs. Jack paid close attention and noticed how one of the rings made her eyes sparkle. It was a square cut sapphire flanked by cabochon rubies, set in a thick band of white gold. It looked both modern and somehow ancient.

"Pretty." Maddie admired it on her hand. "I feel like a Sumerian queen."

Jack glanced at the price, and was suitably impressed. "Shall we take pictures of that one?"

The shop was deserted, and the saleswoman was obliging, so they shot a bunch of pictures and videos, some with her arms around his neck, eyes closed in bliss, the ring on display, some of their hands clasped, some of them kissing with her hand extended, showing the ring off. Jack wanted to buy it for her on the spot, it looked so damn perfect on her hand.

"We'll be back later," Maddie told the saleswoman.

When they returned to the house, Maddie went back to work, and Jack got busy editing the video, glad to have something to keep him busy. He killed another couple of hours looking over material for his business meetings next week, and then it was time to start dinner.

It was twilight when Maddie came out of her cave, drawn by the scent of tangy marinated chicken skewers on the grill outside, accompanied by a tomato and cucumber salad, some fresh, crusty bread from the bakery, and a summer vegetable stew, flavored with marjoram and basil.

When they had finished eating, he spun the laptop around for her.

"I picked the song this time, but I could switch it out for something else if you want," he said. "I used 'Bring the Bling,' It's a new single by Jackhammer, and it's got that gritty, rebellious vibe that you like."

The video opened to a shot of Maddie's slender brown hands, still smeared with ink, and that gorgeous ring, glowing on her finger. Her hands wound around Jack's neck, the ring on full display. Holding him with that hungry grasp, her fingers clutching the nape of his neck, to the wail of the steel guitar, and the singer's rough, resonant baritone voice.

It was earthy, sexy. Anyone watching would envy them. Want to be them.

Damn. He wanted to be them, himself. How twisted in knots was that.

"It's perfect," Maddie said. "Brilliant. Can I post it everywhere?"

"Of course," he said.

She smiled at him. "I think you missed your calling, Jack."

"No," he said flatly. "I found my perfect calling. Someone stole it from me."

That wiped the smile right off her face, to his dismay. *Not classy, Daly.*

"I'm sorry," she said.

"No, I'm the one who should be sorry," he said. "I promised myself not to burden you with my crap, but sometimes it sneaks up on me."

Maddie stood up, looking uncertain. "Well, then. I guess I'll try to get some sleep, so I can get an early start tomorrow. I've still got a lot of work to do. Dinner was delicious. You're a fabulous cook. I'll do the dishes."

"Don't worry, I've got it," he assured her. "I'd rather you spend your time at the whiteboard, doing your magic thing, or else sleeping. Good night."

Jack finished cleaning up the kitchen, and attempted to relax with a shower. But being naked and wet, knowing that she was right through the wall just wound him up more.

He kept seeing that beautiful, long-fingered, ink-stained hand, with the pale gold ring, bright as moonlight against her golden brown skin. It made his chest hurt.

This cycle of emotions was becoming routine. He started to enjoy their playacting just a little too much, and then boom, he crashed and burned, because it wasn't real. And it could never be real.

He had to learn to keep his tender goddamn feelings to himself.

Ten

Maddie spent the next two days studying the BioSpark archives, teasing out every bit of information she could, and plugging it into her own mental matrix.

And after three days, the magic started to happen. Her mind started bubbling up what felt like new information, but which was actually a reworked version of the old.

This was the fun part. The piercing flashes, the aha moments. The excitement.

Problem was, this was the first time that her restless body was getting in the way of the truth by clamoring for its own reward, its own satisfaction, its own agenda.

She was walking a tightrope, because she really, really wanted Jack Daly to be innocent. Not only because of her crush, but just because she simply liked the man. He was funny, smart, his sense of humor matched with hers.

And he was so sexy, it was just outrageous. It shouldn't be allowed.

The overall sense growing inside her was that she didn't believe that Jack would have devalued his own creation enough to sell it out for a flat fee, while also screwing over his best friend and burning his own professional reputation. True, his Energen stock had zoomed up to forty-six million dollars, but that was nothing compared to the billions that BioSpark would have generated for him as the company grew and diversified.

The story of the scam just didn't hold up against their original story of two scrappy young entrepreneurs, putting their hearts and minds into a product that could save the oceans and earn untold billions. The kind of story that inspired Hollywood movies. Compare that to running off to Rio all alone with his ill-gotten gains, having lost all his professional credibility, having betrayed his friends and having sold his life's work to the highest bidder. A traitor, despised by all.

Why would he do that? A man with his talents?

The more she got to know Jack, the more she thought that it wasn't the right question to ask, simply because he hadn't done it. That was the work of a smaller, craftier, more self-serving person. One who cared only for himself.

But dammit, she couldn't expect reality to align with her own personal preferences. That was childish and dangerous. She was afraid to trust her gut on this one.

Jack walked in. "Hey there. Dinner's ready. You hungry?"

"Yeah," she said. "I'm done for tonight."

He walked closer, gazing at her whiteboards covered with a dense scrawl of notes, her fluttering mass of colored sticky notes. "Have you come to any conclusions? Throw me a bone, Maddie."

She hesitated before answering. "Well. If Amelia's data is accurate—"

"It is," Jack said.

"If it's reliable, then I have no doubt that Bio-Spark's research was stolen by Energen," she said. "I've researched the people whose names are on the Energen Vortex project, and I agree with your assessment of their limitations. There's no way those people could have generated that body of work in that time frame, compared to

BioSpark's team and timeline. Plus, in the past year and a half before the IPOs, the big breaks in research for both of the companies start to follow the same arcs, but with a pretty consistent time lag. As if the Energen team were getting regular infusions of information, and then scrambling to incorporate them."

"Yes," Jack said. "Yes, my thoughts exactly."

"So, keeping that in mind, I've been trying to figure out if you were the one to pass them the BioSpark research," Maddie said.

"I see." Jack looked pained. "What did you decide?"

"I'm on shaky ground, here," she admitted. "Because I don't trust my own perceptions when it comes to you. But honestly, Jack? I just don't see you trading what you had with BioSpark for this bullshit." She waved at the whiteboard. "Even if it had worked, and you'd gotten away clean with forty-six million bucks, what's that, compared to BioSpark's potential? You guys would've been billionaires many times over. Famous. Celebrated. Venerated for saving the oceans. People would name libraries and elementary schools after you. You wouldn't trade a lifetime of service to become one of the idle rich, sipping umbrella drinks on a beach. That would bore you to death."

"Not just that," Jack added, his voice rough. "Caleb was family. Your grandmother Elaine was, too. All of you were. And the people at Bio-Spark. They were the only family I had, and I wouldn't have traded that for forty-six million, or forty-six billion. I hope you believe me."

Maddie gazed directly into his eyes, and nodded. "I do believe you, Jack," she said. "God help me, but I do."

Jack closed his eyes, and turned away for a moment. "Thanks." His voice was thick and unsteady. "You can't imagine what that means to me."

Maddie's world was readjusting, recalibrating to this new reality, one in which Jack was innocent. She was still holding both realities suspended in her head: the old one, where Jack was a conniving thief and liar, and the new one, where Jack was just... Jack.

The real, true Jack. The shining truth of him, blazing out of his eyes as he turned to her, wiping away tears that he was too embarrassed to show.

She wiped away her own tears, sniffing aggressively. "Do not make a fool of me, Jack

Daly," she warned him. "Or I will tear you limb from limb."

"I have never been anything but honest with you," Jack said. "I swear to God."

"My one doubt is how badly I want this to be true," she told him. "It makes my judgment suspect."

He took a step toward her. "No," he said. "Your judgment is spot-on."

"I'm still in a bind, though. Unless we can prove your innocence. Because what I've got is subjective. Not solid proof. We need more."

"I know." He touched her cheek with his fingertip, then took her hand, pressing a soft, hot kiss to her palm.

His lips were so warm. She felt the contact throughout her body. Her breath caught, and her thighs clenched around the sweet melting ache of longing.

He felt it. "Oh, man," he said. "We better cool it."

She laughed. "Good luck. Got an ice-cold stream to jump into?"

"Actually, I do," he replied. "Throw on some shoes and a jacket. There's just enough light left tonight to show you one of the waterfalls. The closest one."

Maddie backed away, smiling like a fool, and

retreated to her room. She pulled on her sweat-shirt and her kicks, and tossed her phone on her bed. She wouldn't need it.

She was leaving it all behind. The rest of the world could wait.

She followed him out of the house, and into the forest. Her senses opened up inside her as he led her deeper into the vast cathedral of towering trees, fuzzed with vivid green moss and lichen. The delicate leaves of the foliage at their roots seemed to float in midair. The place hummed and twittered and rustled, fragrant and sweet. It vibrated with life.

And so did she, like never before. Everything she saw and heard and smelled was poignant, charged with brightness. Every tender tree leaf, every crystalline warble of birdsong. Incredible, that this forest had always been exactly this beautiful, exactly this magical—but she hadn't seen it. Hadn't felt it.

Because of Jack, new eyes inside her mind had opened up, and were staring around the world as if she'd never seen it before. Dazzled.

He was so beautiful. Outside, inside. She'd known it all along, since she first met him, but she'd been holding her hands over her eyes, not letting herself see who he really was, because she didn't trust him. Or herself.

Now her doubt was crumbling, her fear lifting. Without it, she felt as light as air. She floated through the hush of the primeval forest with him, awestruck and amazed.

Jack led her to the rocky edge of a canyon. Ice-clear water sluiced through a gleaming chute of water-smoothed granite, and sprayed out onto a rocky downhill slope, creating ethereal bouncing waterfalls all the way down, like a flounced skirt.

"Oh, my God," she said. "All that time, I was in there, guzzling coffee and crunching numbers, while this was outside. This wonderland."

He looked pleased. "You like it? It's one of my favorite places in the world."

"I've never seen anything so beautiful in my life," she told him.

"Me neither," he said quietly. "Until I saw you."

Their hands hung at their sides, but somehow, the outside of her little finger brushed the outside of his, and a sweet thrill of awareness went through her.

Suddenly, their hands were joined, clasped, fingers twined. Her face was so hot, it had to be cherry red. Her heartbeat thrummed, fast and frantic. "Same," she whispered.

He turned to her and took her other hand. "This role-playing we're doing for Elaine," he said. "I want so badly for it to be real."

She gazed up into his eyes. "Me, too."

Then the distance between them closed, and they were kissing.

There was a pleading desperation in the kiss, as if they could be ripped apart at any moment. As if they were gasping for air.

She could have torn off her clothes and had sex with him right there. On the wet stones, bent over a mossy log, pinned against a tree, her bare skin cooled by the misty spray in the waterfall. She felt feverishly hot, straining against that hard bulge against her belly. Melting with readiness.

Jack pulled away. "Back to the house?"

She nodded, and their hands joined again as they walked, though the narrow suggestion of a path really wasn't wide enough for two. Their fingers couldn't let go. They were made to be together, and she'd hungered for that contact, ever since that first kiss at the resort, when the curtain was first torn back on this hunger.

It felt so good, so exquisitely right, to finally give in to it.

The dusk had deepened almost to darkness. There was barely enough light to follow the path, but Jack knew just where he was going, leading her through the gnarled roots of the towering trees, up slopes and back down again. The house came into view, the glass of the long windows glowing in the trees like a dark crystal.

She followed him inside, and they stood there facing each other for a moment in the dimness, locked in a state of wordless, heightened awareness, and anticipation.

There was just enough light to see the somber expression in his eyes. "Maddie," he said. "I want this more than anything I've ever wanted in my life. But once we do this, we can't walk it back. I certainly can't."

"Why would we want to? I want to go forward. With you."

"I just think…" His voice trailed off for a moment, his throat working as he swallowed. "I think that you should think it through. One last time."

She shook her head. "I'm not thinking right now, and I don't miss it one bit. I'm feeling, which I don't usually let myself do. But with you, I can't seem to help it. And I love it, Jack. I love the way this makes me feel. It's…it's just incredible."

"Yes. And this was hard enough when it was just make-believe. But I know how it feels to be exiled from my people. I don't have family left, but BioSpark was my chosen family. To have them turn against me for something bad they thought I'd done—it was terrible, Maddie. Being banished punches a huge hole in your life. You'll always feel it. No matter who you're with, no matter what you're doing, that hole is always there."

She bit her lip to keep it from shaking. "I can make this decision for myself."

"Yes, but you're making the decision blind. You won't know how it feels until you get there." His voice was bleak. "But I do know, Maddie. And I have to tell you."

The pain radiating off him hurt her heart. She stepped forward, putting her hand on his chest. "You're a really good guy, Jack," she whispered.

"You'll be the only one who thinks so," he told her. "My life was totaled, Maddie. I don't want to trash yours, too. You might not feel it now, but you need your people."

She swayed closer to him, placing both hands on his chest, craving his heat and electricity. "Jack," she said simply. "I need you."

"I feel the same way. But unless my name is

cleared, your family will never accept a relation-
ship between us. You know how they feel about
it. Caleb, Elaine, Marcus."

"If they love me, they'll reach out. They'll try
to understand. They have to." She seized a fist-
ful of his shirt, and jerked him closer.

"Whoa!" He laughed under his breath, covering her hands with his. "I'm trying to do the
right thing."

"And I appreciate your gallantry, but you
brought me here, to this magical love nest in the
enchanted woods, and paraded around in front
of me, being sexy and gorgeous, and when I give
in to the temptation, that's when you pull back?
You big tease."

"No, it's not like that. I just want you to remember—"

"No." She stretched up onto her tiptoes, wrapping her arms around his neck. "I don't want to
remember whatever it is. Shut up and kiss me."

Jack let out a low, rasping groan, his arms
around her waist, cupping the back of her head,
his fingers winding into her hair.

She melted. Her eyes, her throat, her heart, between her legs. She went hot and soft and liquid,
surrendering to it completely. All the doubts and
fears and second-guessing were swept away en-

tirely, and all that was left was a desperate need to get closer.

She ached to explore every inch of his skin, the hot taste of his mouth moving on hers, the rasp of his beard scruff against her cheek. To pet the short scrub brush of his hair that was shaved down to nothing at the nape of his neck. To breathe in his scent, spicy and salty and complex. She pawed at the buttons on his shirt before she even knew she was doing it, and he helped her unbutton them.

She laughed when she saw his naked torso, and ran her hands down his chest to his belly with a low, appreciative purring sound.

"What?" he asked. "Do I amuse you?"

"I was thinking about Gabe at the beach the other day," she said. "Running around with his shirt flapping open to show off his abs. He's got nothing on you."

He laughed. "I never thought I'd be competing with Gabe Morehead."

"You aren't. Or rather, he's certainly not competing with you." She stroked her hands down over the silky dark hair on his chest that arrowed down to his belt. She grabbed the buckle, yanking on it. "Get this off."

"Wait. Hold on. Let me catch up," Jack protested.

He lifted up her sweatshirt and tossed it off over her head, and breathed out a sigh of awe as she undid the front snaps of her sports bra, and shrugged it off.

"Oh, Maddie," he said softly. "You're so beautiful. I can hardly breathe."

"I'm very glad you think so, but you should definitely breathe," she told him, popping the buttons of her jeans. "What I have in mind requires lots of oxygen." She stepped out of them and wiggled to get the thong panties down her legs. "Take yours off, too."

Between the two of them, they got rid of his clothes very quickly. The rest of his naked body was as ridiculously gorgeous as his powerful torso. She loved his thickly muscled thighs, his taut ass. The air was goose bumps cool, making his dark nipples taut over his chest muscles, and his body was so hard. So solid and hot against her hand.

And that erection. Ooh la la. World-class. Long and thick and flushed, and so very eager looking. It was hot and hard, pulsing in her grip as she petted him, stroked him.

She felt lit up from the inside, in that breathless confusion of gripping hands, twining legs. Stroking and clutching, madly kissing. His hair was too short to get a grip, but she kept running her hands through it anyway. His long fingers wound into her thick curls, his lips dragging across her skin, his deep voice murmuring something incoherent and desperate between kisses, as his mouth moved to her throat, her shoulder, her breasts.

The sensation was exquisite. He licked and suckled and stroked, drawing out pure pleasure and delight until she felt as if the sun was shining right out of her chest. Her heart burst with it, as the first orgasm rocked her. She threw her head back, clutching the thick, clenched muscles of his back for dear life.

His growl of satisfaction vibrated against her chest, which expanded to make space for everything, everywhere. Endless space. Infinite bliss.

Jack held her until gravity reasserted itself, but when her eyes opened, he sank down to his knees, gripping her hips and kissing her belly. Stroking the small swatch of hair on her mound with his fingertips as he looked up at her.

"Let me taste you," he said roughly.

Speech wasn't an option, so she just gave him a nod, her breath quick and jerky between her trembling lips. She had no idea if she could even handle this voltage.

He pressed his face against her, kissing her, parting her. Sliding his tongue over and around her most sensitive flesh. She clutched his head, pressing herself eagerly against his skillful caresses. It was so perfect, every flick or lick or swirl or slow, tender suckling pull of his tongue… slowly…slowly…over and over…until that vast, obliterating pleasure throbbed through her body once again, and she was lost in sweet oblivion.

This time, she came to her senses in his arms, being carried down the corridor. He pushed the bedroom door open with his foot, and laid her down on the bed.

He climbed on top of her, shielding her from the cold. The cool sheets were a sensual contrast to the intense heat of his big body.

She strained toward him, reaching. Every part of her trying to pull him closer.

Jack reached over her and felt around in a drawer in the bed stand, pulling out a string of condoms. He ripped one off, opened it and rolled it on, then grabbed her hand as he shifted into position between her legs, wrapping her fingers around his broad shaft.

"You put me inside," he said. "At your pace. I won't move until you say."

She wanted to respond, but couldn't. She was in a shivering state of extremity. Sheer, naked need. She wiggled closer, stroking his thick rod against herself. Arching and squirming until she had him right where she craved him. Lodged inside.

She dug her nails into his butt, and pressed him to her. "Now," she begged. "All."

He thrust slowly, deeply inside her, and they both gasped with the intensity of it.

She'd never imagined how wild and out of control she could feel. The limits kept moving, the map kept shifting, the rules changing, and she sobbed with wild eagerness, egging him on with her gasping cries.

His heavy thrusts were exactly what she craved. She wound her legs around him, arching herself to get that perfect sweet sliding pressure, right where she needed it, deep inside, so bright, so slick, so exquisitely good. A honeyed lick of fresh delight inside at every stroke. They strained toward something impossible, inevitable, and it exploded in pure sensation, blasting through them.

And she just knew it. She felt the shining truth of him, and knew that he had never lied to anyone. Which meant that the world was very different than she'd thought.

It was bigger, deeper, wilder, more magical. Infinitely more dangerous.

The stakes had just shot up through the roof—and lost themselves in the stars.

Eleven

Jack buried his nose in her curls, stroking the impossibly smooth skin of her back. Maddie sighed, shifting in his arms and snuggling closer. She dropped a little kiss against his collarbone, and his body stirred. He was stone hard, all over again. Prodding her thigh.

Maddie chuckled lazily when she felt it. "Look at you. Tireless."

"You should talk," he said.

"You inspire me," she told him. "I've never been like this before."

"Like what?"

Maddie's laugh sounded self-conscious. "You know. Jumping you, ripping off your clothes, being a naughty hellcat with voracious sexual needs. You bring it out of me."

That pleased him. It also stimulated him, judging from the stiff, aching state of his hard-on. Maddie shifted with a murmur and reached down, idly stroking him. Squeezing.

"Like titanium," she murmured. "Ready for more?"

"I don't want to overdo it for you," he said.

"I'm just fine, thank you very much." There was laughter in her voice.

She moved over him, stretching across his body to the bedside table and groping until she found the condoms, ripping one of the foil packets open. "I see you were prepared for anything, hmm?"

"I actually didn't stock that drawer," he told her. "That was my landlady, Delilah. It's her sexy little joke. She thinks I should get more action, so she always loads up the drawer with condoms when I come here, and then teases me about it."

"Ah," she murmured. "That's cute. Weird and inappropriate, but cute."

"Yeah, she's a salty dog. A whole lot of fun. I've been coming here for years, and we're old friends... Oh. Whoa." His words cut off in a gasp as Maddie rolled the condom over him, with a long, tight, possessive squeezing stroke. "Oh, God, Maddie."

"Too hard?" she asked, with another slow, expert twist of her hand...and again.

"Slow down, or I'll lose it," he said, his voice strangled.

"Oh, we can't have that. First you must attend to my insatiable appetites."

"Can I turn on the light?" he asked her. "You're so beautiful. I want to see it all."

She hesitated, for just a moment, and then nodded. Jack flicked on the bedside light to its lowest setting. A gentle glow, like candlelight. They smiled at each other.

"Happy now?" she asked.

"Ecstatic," he assured her. "Fulfillment of insatiable appetites, coming right up."

She laughed. "It certainly has come right up," she said appreciatively, swinging her shapely thigh over him. Swaying and undulating as she stroked his stiff phallus, then lifting herself up to nudge him slowly inside.

He gasped as she sank down, taking him so deep. Hot, tight, plush. Clinging.

She grabbed one of his hands, putting it against her mound. "Touch me again, like you did in my room at the resort," she said, her voice breathless. "I loved that."

Oh, yeah. Caressing the taut, sensitive nub between her tender folds while she rode him, rising and falling, breasts bouncing…that was his idea of earthly paradise.

Her face was dewy and flushed, eyes dazzled with pleasure. So beautiful. Her first orgasm came quickly. He was glad the light was on. He loved how she looked, gasping for breath, head thrown back. Those sexy sounds she made.

He kept at it, making her come yet again…and again. After that, she leaned over him, wordlessly demanding with her body that this time, he follow her. All the way to the explosive end.

God, yes. He held her, pumping up into her body. The deep, surging rhythm intensified… and they were swept away, lost in the surging waves of sensation…and tossed up on some distant shore afterward, dazed and exhausted.

A while later, she lifted her head. "The last thing I want to do now is move a single muscle. But you'd better do something about that condom."

"Yeah, that would be smart." He held it as she lifted herself off, and went to the bathroom to dispose of it. He splashed his face, irrationally afraid that she would vanish if he took his eyes off her. Something this good just didn't belong in his raggedy, cobbled-together life. And knowing what Caleb and Marcus and Elaine thought of him, it almost felt as if he were stealing for real. Something far more precious than money or IP.

When he came out of the bathroom, he just stood there for a while, dazed by her smile. Her intelligent, beautiful golden eyes, so full of light.

Then something occurred to him: his duty as a host. "Hey," he said. "You know what? I cooked dinner for you, and we forgot all about it."

Her eyes widened. "Oh, dear. I hope it didn't burn."

"No, it's just waiting for us in there on the table. Are you hungry?"

"At this hour?"

He glanced at the clock. "A midnight feast. Seems appropriate."

"Give me a couple of minutes in the bathroom, and I'll be right in," she said. "My appetite just woke up. That appetite, anyway. Others have been raging ever since…well."

"Since when?" he asked, intrigued.

"Truthfully?" She let out a soft laugh. "Do you remember that time you came to the lake with

Caleb, the summer after you graduated from high school?"

His mouth dropped open. "No way! You were just a little kid!"

"Not really. Almost fourteen. Old enough to notice a gorgeous guy in swim trunks, dripping wet, full of muscle. Old enough to pine for him."

"Um…wow," he said, bemused. "And I had no clue."

There was an awkward pause, and Maddie waved it away. "Sorry. I didn't mean to put you on the spot or make you feel weird. Perved on by the youthful, teenage me."

"Oh, no," he said. "I just can't believe that I never noticed."

"Thank God," she said. "I would've died of embarrassment."

"Well, you're not embarrassed now, are you?"

"Nope." She gave him that smoldering stare, and his body reacted predictably.

Maddie laughed, scooping up his jeans and flinging them at him. "Feed me before you raise the flag again, buddy."

"Oh, yeah. Of course. I'll be in the kitchen. See you there."

She disappeared into the bathroom, throwing a seductive smile over her shoulder, while a dazed, flustered Jack stumbled into the kitchen, pulling his wits together.

The necessary sequence of events was simple. Wrap up the barbecued ribs in foil. Stick them into the oven to warm. Heat up the spiced potatoes, peppers and sweet red onions in the big cast-iron skillet. Throw a handful of shredded pepper jack cheese on top to melt. Toss the salad greens with vinaigrette. Pull out a couple of local beers.

"You live dangerously," said Maddie's teasing voice from behind him. "Cooking, naked to the waist? Shouldn't you at least wear an apron? I bet that would look kinky and fetishistic on you, with all those tight, cut muscles you've got."

"I'm not frying bacon." He gave her a grin. "Besides, you've jacked up my temperature permanently by a couple of degrees. I'm not cold at all."

"Me neither." She walked into the kitchen, wearing one of his T-shirts. It had slid off her golden brown shoulder. "I swiped one of your shirts," she said. "Hope it's okay."

"It looks awesome on you," he told her.

She gave him a smile that made him forget his own name. He fought to get his mind back on track. "Uh… I have beer, if you want," he said, holding out the bottle to her. "A very good local brew. Or else there's wine. White or red. Whatever you prefer."

"Beer's fine." She took the bottle.

He'd set the table hours ago, in preparation for the dinner they had forgotten to eat, so all that was left was to open the foil on the steaming, tender meat and slide the packet onto a serving plate. He placed the sizzling potato, pepper and onion concoction onto the table, put down the salad bowl, and pried open the tops of their beers. "To us," he said.

They clicked bottles, and drank.

"Oh, that's good," she said with a sigh. "The food smells divine. I've been enjoying your cooking. I'm not a bad cook myself, but oh, do I love being cooked for."

"It's my pleasure," he assured her.

They devoured dinner. He didn't remember having an appetite this keen since he was a teenager. When they slowed down, they exchanged almost guilty looks.

"I don't think I've ever pigged out like this in my entire life," Maddie said.

"We worked up an appetite."

"I can't believe how much fun I'm having," she said. "I've been so wound up for such a long time now. And suddenly, kaboom. Here's you, unraveling me."

"You're having the same effect on me, too," he admitted. "I can breathe, for the first time in forever. This is the best thing that has ever happened to me."

"Same." Maddie lifted her beer bottle. "To the truth," she said.

"To the truth," he echoed.

They clinked bottles and drank as an odd thought formed in his mind. "This is the first time I've ever seen any sense in my misfortune," he said. "A larger design."

"What kind of design?" she asked.

Jack had to think carefully before he could put it into words. "If all that bad stuff hadn't happened nine years ago, I'd be in a different place right now," he said. "I'd be a tech mogul, running BioSpark with Caleb, which would have grown tenfold. I'd probably be married to Gabriella. I'd already given her a ring, back before it all happened."

"A ring? Did she send it back to you when she dumped you?"

Jack shook his head, lips twitching. "Not a freaking chance," he said. "Not her."

"That's grasping," Maddie said. "She gives women a bad name."

"Anyhow, my point is, I would've been married for seven or eight years, so probably we would have had a couple of kids by now. My life would have gone down that path, and I'd be a million miles from here. I would not be in this kitchen, eating a midnight feast with Maddie Moss, who's dressed in my T-shirt."

"And absolutely nothing else," she added.

That made his groin tighten. "Really?"

"Absolutely," Maddie said, rucking up the bottom of the shirt with a teasing finger to give him a brief glimpse of the shadowy glories beneath. "But by all means, finish your thought. We'll get back to that little detail later."

"Ah…yeah," he said. "Anyhow. I was just thinking that if all that crap was the only path toward this moment, then it was worth it. Just this, right now, with you. The way you make me feel." He shrugged. "It's worth it, to me. Worth any price."

"Oh, Jack," she said. "That's such a sweet thought, but I would never want you to pay so high a price for anything."

"It doesn't matter," he said philosophically. "We don't get to choose."

Maddie gazed at him, chewing her lip, a thoughtful little frown between her brows.

"I don't see it that way," she said. "We're always making choices, going through this door rather than that door. Every choice has its gifts, and its price, too. If you'd married Gabriella and had kids with her, and even if for some reason it hadn't worked out with her, still you'd love those kids with all your heart and soul. You wouldn't be able to imagine the world without them. For that reason, it would've been worth it, and you'd be committed to it. Anything you might have gone through would've been worth it because your kids would have been the gift of that particular timeline."

"Maybe you're right," he said. "But in this timeline? I am so incredibly glad that I did not marry Gabriella Adriani."

Maddie's long lashes fell, veiling her eyes. "Me, too."

"I like the idea of having kids, and loving them with all my heart and soul," he went on. "But Gabriella is not the woman that I want to have them with."

She slanted him a stern look. "Jack. We're getting ahead of ourselves."

"Probably," he admitted. "Sorry. You have that effect on me."

Maddie waved that away. "I used to think, for instance, suppose my mother had decided not to get on that yacht, on that particular day. Would my life have been different, ultimately? She still would have sent me to Gran, once she got bored with having a toddler around. I'd just have a different set of psychological complexes, brought on by a lifetime of trying to get the attention of a woman whose only interest was in herself. Instead, I got Gran, who is intensely interested in me and my potential. It's maddening, either way."

"You don't think certain things are destined to be?" he asked. "Children, lovers, the hour of your death? All that big stuff?"

She shook her head. "No. It's chance, it's choice. An unpredictable blend of the two."

As he thought about chance and choice and destiny, he couldn't help imagining kids that were a blend of him and Maddie. What they might look like, and be like.

Dial it down, boy. You're a long way from the finish line. Dad's gruff voice.

Maddie stood up, walking slowly around the table toward him. "Jack."

"Yeah?"

"I have a contraceptive implant," she said. "And on my last checkup, I had no diseases of any kind. What about you? What's your status?"

His heart practically stuttered with excitement at the implications of her remark. "No diseases at all," he said. "But I can't believe you'd trust me that much."

She gave him a sweet, open smile. "Well, believe it. You've convinced me."

"I... I don't know what to say."

She took his hand, sliding it under the front of the T-shirt. Such fine skin. Flower-petal soft. "I didn't ask you to say anything," she whispered. "Just touch me."

He caressed her, expertly, fingers sliding with such unerring skill around her hidden folds, circling and stroking and driving her mad. It wasn't long before they were stumbling back to the bedroom, kissing wildly.

He let go of her just long enough to drop his sweatpants, peel off her T-shirt and tumble back onto the bed with her. Both of them ravenous for that feeling, that magic fusion. He was addicted to it. The sense of new beginnings, infinite possibilities.

They wrapped around each other's bodies, giving in to a surging rhythm. Melting into each other as extreme pleasure welled up through them, pulsing up so deep, it wiped out all thought. Wordless, timeless. Perfect.

When he came back to waking consciousness, his eyes were wet. Already, he felt cold reality encroaching on this miraculous thing. Threatening it from every side.

Maddie stirred next to him, lifting her head with a frown. "Jack? You okay?"

"Fine," he said.

"So why do you look so sad?"

He shook his head, not wanting to invite the dangers any closer by naming them, but Maddie patted his chest insistently. "Tell me," she said.

He let out a sigh. "There's a good chance that we'll never find an iron-clad way to prove to Caleb and your grandmother that I'm innocent," he admitted.

"We'll cross that bridge when we come to it," Maddie said.

"No, actually. You should think about that bridge before."

"Just keep a positive outlook," she urged. "We'll find a way somehow. Together."

Jack winced. "A positive outlook means nothing," he said. "When you lose something precious, it's gone. A parent or a grandparent, a company, a lover, your reputation, your career, whatever it is, it's gone. You grieve it, you learn to live without it, but your life is smaller afterward. There are consequences to everything. You just can't see them yet. Elaine is old. You don't want to be estranged from her."

"Gran is not helpless," Maddie said sharply. "She could meet me halfway if she cared more about me than being right. She's no frail, helpless victim. She's a powerful person who can make her own choices." Maddie jerked up onto her elbow and glared at him. "And I do not think that being with you will make my life smaller."

"I really hope that's true," he said.

Maddie waved her arm, sharply. "So, what are you telling me? That we made a mistake, that you've changed your mind? That you're sorry we did this?"

"God, no," he said. "I said it's worth any price to me, and I mean it. I just don't want you to pay the price, too. I wish I could spare you that."

"I appreciate the thought, but I can take responsibility for my own choices," she said. "We'll find a way to fix this, Jack. I want to rewrite the script."

He laughed under his breath. "Easy for you to

say," he said. "You're a Moss. You're accustomed to being the master of all that you survey. Caleb was like that, too."

"You think?" she said. "Being Susanna Moss's daughter has been no bed of roses, Jack. I don't even know my father's name, let alone bear it. Remember how Bruce threw that in my face? A defect he was willing to overlook. How magnanimous of him."

"Dickhead," he muttered.

"Pretty much, but the point is, I've been driven to excel at all costs, and that twists you up inside," she said. "Gran feels guilty about driving us and stressing us to achieve in our careers at the expense of our personal lives, which is why now she's trying to overcompensate for that with this stupid marriage mandate. I've had her controlling me and breathing down my neck and lecturing me my whole life. I love the woman, but my God. She definitely screwed us all up, each in our own special way."

"You seem perfect to me," he said. "Kissed by fate. You have beauty, brains, heart. Loads of charisma. A sense of humor. Courage. Compassion. Glamour. Luck."

"That's so sweet," she told him. "But you have all those things, too."

"Maybe not the luck," he said wryly.

"Oh, no?" Maddie climbed on top of him again. "Really, Jack?" She reached down, caressing his stiff, aching penis with a snug, expert swirl of her hand. "Look me in the eye and tell me you don't feel lucky right now."

He was about to reply, but then Maddie sank down and pulled him in her hot, teasing mouth… and he could no longer speak at all.

Twelve

Maddie felt the faint light of dawn pressing against her eyes. She was floating on air. Soft, pliant. Weightless. When she opened her eyes, there was Jack, next to her.

So it wasn't a dream.

He was so beautiful, it hurt to look at him. She studied his beard stubble, the sweeping line of his dark eyebrows. The ridiculous thickness of his black eyelashes. His mouth was relaxed, sensual, like she remembered him as a boy. It was so tight and sealed when he was awake. Always braced for whatever the world might throw at him.

His eyes opened, just a slit, and he grinned.

"Is this real?" His voice was a sleepy rasp. "Or am I still dreaming?"

"I'll seem real enough when I start getting way up in your face," she teased. "I'm no fantasy woman. I have my fatal flaws. Give me time. You'll see."

"Take all the time you want," he said. "Forever."

Maddie blinked at him, eyes wide. "Um…."

"Oh, crap," he muttered, rolling onto his back and clapping his hand over his eyes. "I'm overdoing it again, right? Getting ahead of myself?"

"Little bit," she admitted. "But I'm handling it. You're just…very intense."

"I know," he said wryly. "It's just really hard for me to keep it light. After last night, it's going to be even harder."

"I know." She leaned over to look at his clock. "It's late," she said. "Lolling in bed with you is my new favorite thing in the world to do, but it's Saturday. Ava's wedding is at the Triple Falls Lodge at five this evening, and it's way up in the mountains. I have a room already reserved, but if we want to get there in time to check in and freshen up, we have to get moving."

"Do you need to stop at your place in Seattle first?"

"Not if I recycle a dress from last weekend."

Jack's eyes lit up. "The blue halter dress?"

Maddie smiled. "Oh, you like that one? Good. It's a favorite of mine."

"I love that one," he said. "You look like a goddess from Mount Olympus."

"Okay, then. I think that dress is still in wearable shape, so there's no need to stop at my house in Seattle," she said briskly. "Excellent. We should still get going, though."

"You shower while I make some coffee," he suggested. "Breakfast?"

"Let's grab it on the road."

In less than an hour, they were showered, dressed, bags by the door, sipping coffee. Maddie looked around at the mess from last night's feast, completely forgotten in the throes of passion. "Shall we take a moment to get the kitchen in order before we go?"

"No, I've texted Delilah, and told her to send the cleaning service," he said. "They'll take care of it. Let's get on the road."

Jack insisted on taking the first turn at driving, and paying for gas. But when these details were dealt with and they were sailing down the highway, he fell silent.

There had been many types of silence between them. This one wasn't at all like yesterday's silence, in the woods, when they'd walked together in perfect shining communion, their minds so linked there was simply no need to speak.

This silence was a wall. She tried to make conversation, several times, but all her attempts fell flat.

Finally, Maddie gathered her nerve. "Jack, what the hell?" she demanded.

"What?" He looked over at her, bewildered. "What's wrong?"

"Why the grim silence? Did I piss you off somehow?"

Jack looked horrified. "No! I had the best night of my life last night. You're amazing."

"Then what the hell is the problem?"

Jack looked hunted. "That *is* the problem, Maddie. How perfect it was."

Maddie gave him a narrow look. "Dude. You've lost me. Orient me, in your maze of a brain."

"Hell, I don't know." Jack shook his head. "This time with you…it's like a magic bubble, and now it's about to pop. We're going back into the real world, so I'm getting defensive and uptight. That's all this is. Please don't take it personally."

Maddie reached over and placed her hand on his knee. "That magic bubble hasn't broken with me," she told him. "I believe in you, Jack."

Jack laid his hand on hers. "Thanks. But it's weird, because I'm not sure what part I'm supposed to play today. The unscrupulous bad boy who's cruelly toying with you in order to drive your family to the brink, or..."

"Or what?" she demanded.

He let out a sigh. "Or the guy who's head over ass in love with you for real. Engaged to you for real. Making love to you, all night, every night, for the rest of our lives for real. How do I sort that out? It's tying me in knots."

Maggie stared at his stark profile for a long moment. She was digging her nails into his thigh, hard enough to leave marks, but he didn't seem to notice.

Jack was right. They were at a crossroads. Her heart was dragging her like a team of wild horses, right toward what must look like a cliff, from the outside. Doom, in plain sight. Very hard to explain to people who couldn't possibly understand.

But the alternative was to close her heart down.

Turn away from him. Stay in the suffocating gray zone, where she was frustrated, stifled, bored to death.

"It only matters to the two of us, ultimately," Jack mused. "Our behavior in either scenario is the same. But after what happened between us last night, I can't pretend to fake something that's so incredibly real to me. I just want to live this. Fully and honestly, like a normal person with normal feelings. Do you see my dilemma?"

"Yes," she said, and in a split second, her decision just made itself. "I think we should go for it. Feel what we feel, and act accordingly."

Jack gave her a wry look. "That's too cryptic for me," he said. "Be clearer."

"Clear how? What should we do, then? Make a formal declaration to each other?"

"I'm game," Jack said swiftly. "If you think it would help."

"Well, okay," she said, uncertainly. "Clarity is always good, right?"

Without saying another word, Jack flipped on the turn signal, and directed the car onto the next off-ramp. They got off the highway, cruising along until they found themselves on a side road through some alfalfa fields, bordered by a swampy little creek.

Jack pulled over. Thick green grass swished the car's undercarriage. "Let's go."

"What in the world are we doing here?" Maddie asked.

He gave her a blinding grin. "Seeking clarity."

Once outside the car, he took her hand and led her out into a field, near a stock pond where a weeping willow tree stood. The ground was boggy, thick with weeds and cattails. Cows gazed over the fence at them with mild curiosity.

"Jack, what the hell?" she asked, baffled.

"We're here for the tree," he said, gesturing at the willow. "I was looking for an appropriate setting for this declaration. On such short notice, this is the best I can do. It's definitely not something a man can do while driving on the interstate."

"Oh," she murmured. "Ah...this is a little more than I bargained for."

But Jack was undeterred. "Madelyn Moss, I don't look great on paper right now, but my heart is yours completely. I see what you are, and I love it." He sank down into the wet grass onto one knee. "I wish I had a ring, but this is my formal declaration of intent. Let me love you for the rest of our lives. Please. Marry me."

Maddie's eyes filled. Her free hand had floated up to hide her shaking mouth. Her heart galloped. "I thought, um…that couples got to this place gradually," she faltered.

"Sure, in the normal world. But our lives aren't normal. And sometimes, you just have to take your shot." Jack kissed her hand. "You don't dare let it slip away."

She looked down at his warm hand enveloping hers. His beautiful eyes, blazing at her. Expectant. Hopeful. It was like looking into the sun.

"Jack, you are a piece of work," she whispered.

"You're pretty damn memorable yourself, babe. And you know? Even apart from the fireworks, and outrageously good sex, I think we make a pretty good team."

She kept trying to reply, but the words wouldn't come out.

Then Jack gave her a smile so sweet, it made her breath catch. "I get it," he said gently. "You don't have to answer now. I'm rushing you. You're just so amazing, I lost my head. We can save this for later. My feelings won't go away."

He kissed her hand again, and got up, brushing at the muddy splotch on the knee of his jeans.

"I guess we should get back on the road, if the wedding is at—"

"Yes," she burst out.

Jack's eyes narrowed, uncertain. "You mean, yes, let's get back on the road?"

"No, I mean, yes to the fireworks, and the outrageously good sex, and to being a team. Yes, to taking our shot. Yes, to all that. Yes, yes, yes."

Jack's eyes lit up, and they came together, kissing again like the fate of the world depended on it. The long, swaying willow fronds were a magical bower—

Beep. Beeeeep.

They jerked around, startled. An old green Ford pickup was lumbering along the raggedy asphalt road. An old man with a visored cap was driving, and his wife sat beside him, tight-lipped, helmet-haired, wearing schoolmarmish glasses. The old couple stared at them with obvious disapproval, slowing almost to a stop. *Beeeeep,* one last time, and then the woman said something sharp to the man, and the pickup accelerated away.

"Maybe it's his stock pond," Jack said. "I guess that's our cue. Shall we pick this up again in the hotel room at the Triple Falls Lodge? Exactly where we left off?"

"I'm counting on it," she said.

"This is real, right?" he asked her. "I'm not dreaming, or hallucinating?"

"I said yes," she told him. "I said it emphatically. I made a formal declaration. We can both be crystal clear when we put our minds to it."

They squelched through the mud and the boggy grass, hands clasped, smiling helplessly at each other. They got into the car, and he looked over at her.

"I'm floating," he said. "Three feet in the air."

"Sounds distracting. Want me to drive?"

He laughed at her as he started up the engine. "Nah, I'm still functional. It's just been so long since I felt this way, you know? Hell, maybe I've never felt this good. This is sky opening up, blaze-of-glory-type happiness."

"Me, too," she said softly.

They got back onto the highway, and Maddie found a radio station. She stopped when she heard the opening guitar riff for the Jackhammer song, "Bring the Bling."

"That reminds me," Jack said. "The ring. We're going to Ava Maddox's wedding, formally engaged, and you've got no ring."

Maddie shrugged. "So we're getting it sized, or something."

"I believe one of your hashtags was #ItFits-Perfectly."

She shrugged. "Who cares? We're no longer putting on an act, so we no longer need to worry about looking authentic. We're real. People can think what they want."

"God knows, they will anyway," he said.

The song lyrics suddenly came to the foreground when they fell silent. The singer's deep, scratchy baritone voice punched the words out to the heavy beat.

I don't care what the haters think,
I just do my thing.
Let them cut and spit and stab,
But I still bring the bling,
Yeah I always bring the bling.

She felt the shift in Jack's mood, as if the sun had gone behind a cloud. He took his hand away to switch on the turn signal, passed the truck, and then left his hand on the steering wheel afterward. He didn't put it back on hers.

Her own hand felt lonely. Longing for his touch.

They were barreling into the thick of it now. The real world, people they both knew, with their strong opinions and their prejudices. Haters gotta hate, and they just had to keep doing their thing, no matter what.

But Jack was dreading it. And she didn't blame him.

Thirteen

"Stunning," Jack said, from where he lay still lounging on the bed, naked and relaxed.

Maddie slowly turned in front of the full-length mirror on the wall, showing him every angle of the pale blue backless halter dress as she studied herself critically.

They had gotten to Triple Falls Lodge and checked into Maddie's room without seeing anyone they knew, and he was grateful. He'd have to face all of them eventually, but he just wasn't ready to give up this euphoric feeling yet.

It felt so good, but it could be crushed with a curt word, an ugly laugh. And there he'd be again, fending off shame for a thing he had not done. Rage, for the unfairness.

Stop. He couldn't let his toxic shame-and-rage crap anywhere near Maddie. She didn't deserve it. She was a miracle.

"You should grab a shower," she told him. "We don't have much time left."

"I still can't move," he drawled. "You drained all my strength. I'm spent. And besides, you're so damn beautiful when you're getting dressed. How can I look away from that?"

"Aww." Maddie gave him a sultry smile as she fastened a pair of glittering drop earrings, and then positioned a square cut aquamarine on a ribbon around her throat. The stones caught the light, glowing against her gorgeous golden brown skin. Then she twisted up her curls into a high French roll, fastening it with an aquamarine clip.

She looked like a Greek goddess. The long, finely pleated skirt skimmed her perfect curves, the crisscrossed bodice cradled her full, gorgeous breasts. The dress was braless, backless, but she tossed a stole over her shoulders. It was the same pale blue on the inside, and a deeper, stormy blue on the outside.

"If you're not ready in five minutes, I'm going down alone," she warned.

He slid reluctantly out of bed, enjoying her appreciative eyes on his naked body. "I'll be quick," he assured her.

"Hey," she said. "You don't have to do this, understand? It's not required."

"But I promised. We had a deal."

"That was before, when it was all theater, to shock Gran," she pointed out. "We're past that now. So if you don't want to deal with all of them today, don't come down. I'll join you afterward. It's fine. Really."

Jack was tempted for a moment, but he shook his head. "I can't start our life together as a couple cowering in a hotel room."

Her dazzling smile was his reward. "Well, hurry, then."

Jack showered and shaved, donned the shirt and suit that he'd gotten cleaned and pressed last week in Cleland, slid on his dress shoes, all in record time, then smiled and offered her his arm. He had a lump of sick dread in his belly, but he wasn't going to burden her with it. He'd just brazen it out, and act like any other insanely lucky man who found himself engaged to a brilliant, sexy bombshell of a woman.

His good luck far outweighed the bad.

Downstairs in the big, turn-of-the-century mansion, there were signs pointing to the flower-decked hall where the wedding would take place. They took the seats close to the back, so they weren't immediately noticed. Which made him hope that he might slide through this entire event unobserved. That it might not be as bad as he'd feared.

The enormous wood-paneled room glowed with light from tall, arched windows, and was filling with people, all dressed to the nines. The groom, Zack Austin, was a tall, tux-clad guy with short dark hair whom Jack remembered seeing at parties long ago. He waited at the flowery, beribboned arbor at the front, flanked by two men Jack also knew. One was Drew Maddox, Ava's older brother, an architect, and the other was Vann Acosta. Both of them worked at Maddox Hill, the famous architecture firm founded by Drew's uncle. Drew was the CEO and Vann was the CFO. He'd met them through Ava, back when she'd done some PR work for BioSpark.

A string quintet swelled, playing the wedding march, and they twisted around to see the grizzled, white-haired Malcolm Maddox, Drew and Ava's uncle, walking slowly up the aisle, one hand clutching his cane, and the other clutching Ava's arm. He frowned fiercely, but his eyes were suspiciously shiny, and he kept dabbing his nose with a tissue.

Ava looked as stunning as ever. Her face shone with happiness, and her hair was a loose mass of honey-blond curls. Her long white dress was deceptively simple and low-cut, showing off her stunning body. Her eyes were also wet. She carried a big sheaf of bright sunflowers.

She was followed up the aisle by two extremely good-looking women. Jack vaguely remembered the cute, curly redhead, who was visibly pregnant. Jenna was her name. Ava's best buddy. Some sort of engineer. He'd heard that she'd gotten married to Drew.

The other woman was a tall, beautiful brunette he'd never seen before.

So Drew was going to be a father. Jack was assailed with a sudden image of Maddie pregnant, and got zapped by a feeling so powerful, he had to shut it down.

Now was not the time to be vulnerable and naked. He needed full battle armor.

Maddie leaned over to whisper to him. "The brunette is Sophie, Malcolm's long-lost daughter, and Ava and Drew's cousin. She and Vann

Acosta fell in love last year. It's a crazy story. Remind me to tell it to you sometime."

"Sure. Can't wait." Right now, he was a fan of crazy, romantic stories. The more improbable they were, the better. He needed all the hope he could get.

The ceremony went smoothly, and was charged with emotion. There were readings, and a sermon, of which he didn't understand a word. The bridesmaids and the groomsmen all read carefully chosen poetry about love and trust and commitment. And in the middle of the brunette's reading from the Song of Solomon, Drew spotted him.

His smile faded. His face froze, and he nudged the guy next to him. Vann followed his friend's gaze, and his eyes locked with Jack's. Vann's face hardened, too.

Jack realized that with one slick move, he could create a big, unpleasant scene and mar Ava's wedding. He'd been so focused on himself. Ava was one of the nicest people he knew. She did not deserve to have her big day upstaged by his toxic crap.

Then Malcolm Maddox noticed him, too. Jack had met Malcolm at parties, galas. The old man glared at him, but the ceremony went on, the bride and groom oblivious in their incandescent happiness. They were pronounced man and wife, and they came together in a passionate kiss, arms wound around each other. The room erupted in wild applause.

Ava and her guy were so happy to be kissing each other, they had clearly forgotten the existence of hundreds of hooting, cheering people around them. Which was exactly how Maddie made him feel. Ava and this Zack guy...they had no idea how lucky they were. The whole damn world approved of their love. Applauded it.

Stop feeling sorry for yourself, boy. You're luckier than most men ever dream of.

It was Dad's gruff tone in his head again, always keeping him honest. Jacking up the armor he'd developed long ago, first in the foster homes where he'd landed after Dad's sudden death. He'd perfected it during his trial, and his hellish stint in prison.

Shoulders back, head up, back straight. He was Maddie Moss's fiancé. He had nothing to be ashamed of. His force field was up, buzzing hot, full strength.

But it wasn't enough for him to face the receiving line. Maddie could run that gauntlet on her own.

Jack retreated to a library at the end of the hall, steeling his nerves for the clashes that would come next. The view from the library was beautiful. The sun was setting, and snowcapped Mount Rainier reared up, glowing golden against the fading sky. The trees were thick and dark on the steep, shadowed slopes. He gazed at the mountain, letting it steady him.

"Jack?"

He turned at Maddie's voice. Her graceful figure was silhouetted against the light from the glittering Belle Epoque chandelier in the hall outside. "What are you doing in here?" she asked.

"Recharging," he told her. "This situation burns up a lot of juice."

She walked in. "I noticed Drew and Vann and Malcolm were looking at you."

"I noticed, too," he said.

"Jack, like I said, you don't have to—"

"Maddie? Are you in here?"

They spun around to see a tall, gorgeous redheaded woman in a dark green sheath dress at the door.

"Ronnie?" Maddie said. "Yes, I'm here."

"Did I really see you sitting with—" Veronica Moss's voice trailed off, as her eyes adjusted, and she saw Jack. "Oh. So it's true."

"You know my cousin Veronica, right, Jack?" Maddie kept her voice cheerful and normal, as if Ronnie's eyes weren't full of confusion and dread at the sight of him.

"Yes, I believe we've met," Jack said. "You're the one who hosts that show, *The Secret Life of Plants*, right? Very smart, beautiful show. My compliments."

Ronnie folded her arms over her chest, her green eyes narrowed. "Thanks," she said coolly. "Could you give Maddie and me a moment alone, please?"

"Sure," he said, but Maddie grabbed his arm.

"No," Maddie said. "Anything you have to say can be said in front of my fiancé."

"Oh, God," Ronnie said. "So you're doing this, for real? Gran was supposed to come to this wedding, did you know that? But she didn't. She's too stressed and exhausted. And my dad keeps calling her to gloat, the bastard. Which doesn't help."

"I was under the impression that she didn't intend to come to this event," Maddie said stiffly. "And I'm very sorry that she's finding the consequences of her own actions to be so unpleasant. I'm just living my life, Ron."

"We know why you're doing it, Mads, but

you've gone too far with this charade." Ronnie's voice was low and impassioned. "You're hurting Gran and Caleb for real, and that's not like you. I understand that you want to shock her. I get where you're coming from. But waving the nuclear option, at your own grandmother?"

"Nuclear option, huh?" Jack murmured. "Harsh."

"I asked for privacy," Ronnie retorted. "You wouldn't give it to me. I didn't ask for your input, so please shut up."

"It's not a charade, Ron," Maddie said.

Ronnie's eyes were big and shocked. Her mouth dropped open. "Not a charade?" She faltered. "Then…what the hell is it? What the hell are you doing?"

"Exactly what it looks like we're doing," Maddie said. "Jack and I are together. We're engaged. He's innocent, Ronnie. He didn't do what he was accused of doing. And I'm going to help him prove it."

Ronnie clapped her hand over her mouth. "Oh, no," she whispered. "You can't let him get to you like that. He's scamming you."

"I didn't 'get to' anyone," Jack said, though he knew it was futile.

"Don't speak of him in that way," Maddie said

sternly. "He's my future husband, and I won't let anyone bad-mouth him."

"This is so much worse than we thought," Ronnie said. "You're not just punishing Gran. You're genuinely in love. With Jack-freaking-Daly. God, Mads!"

"Ron, you know me," Maddie coaxed. "Trust me. I'm not stupid, or gullible. I studied the data. If you had studied it, you would've come to the same conclusion. Please, just give us the benefit of the doubt, until I can find some hard proof. I swear to you, the BioSpark thing didn't happen the way they said. Let me explain how the—"

"No." Ronnie backed away. "I'm not joining you in fantasy land."

"But it's not true!" Maddie wailed. "None of it is true! He was set up!"

"I can't. I'm sorry." Ronnie ran out of the room.

Maddie flinched as the library door banged shut. Jack put his hand on the hot, smooth skin of her shoulder, and she jerked back at his touch. He lifted his hand away.

"Shall we take a break?" he asked her gently. "Go up to the room for a while?"

She nodded. Jack put his arm around her and led her out of the library, calculating the closest stairwell with the lowest probability of encountering other wedding guests.

No such luck. Just a few feet from the stairwell, Drew Maddox and Vann Acosta emerged from the ballroom, their faces grim with resolve.

They blocked their path to the stairwell. Maddie clutched his arm.

He repeated the mantra in his head. *Shoulders back. Head up. No shame.*

"I don't know what the hell you think you're doing here," Drew said, his voice low and furious. "But my little sister's wedding is not the place to do it."

"Drew, he's my plus-one," Maddie explained. "Jack's my new fiancé, and I—"

"And you!" Drew turned his thunderous gaze on her. "I thought you were Ava's friend. And mine."

"I am your friend," Maddie protested.

"Really? So you bring your family's big ugly drama to play out at Ava's wedding? That's selfish, Maddie. And sloppy."

She rocked back, startled. "Drew, I never meant to—"

"Fine. You didn't mean to. Good to know. I'll give you the benefit of the doubt, if he leaves right now, before Ava notices you two together.

The Moss family's weird dynamics are not what she should be thinking about today. Understand?"

"Perfectly," Jack said quietly. "Just step out of our way, and I'm gone."

Drew gave him a curt nod, and stepped to the side.

Jack took Maddie's arm, and tugged on it. She drifted alongside him, looking lost.

The stairwell was mercifully close, and once inside the door, he resisted the urge to hug her right there. She needed the privacy of a locked room.

They climbed the stairs to the third floor, and made their way to the room. Once inside, he led her over to the bed and sat down next to her, twining his fingers through hers. They sat in silence for several minutes.

A big shudder racked her. She finally spoke. "God, Jack. That was awful."

He nodded, squeezing her hand. "Welcome to my world."

She looked at him, her eyes wide and wet, and pulled a tissue from her bag, wiping the teary smears of mascara with it. "Really?" she whispered. "It's like that?"

"Yes," he said. "With anyone who knew me

from that time. And that's a lot of people. Caleb and I were pretty notorious, back in the day."

"Yes, I remember all the magazine covers," Maddie said. "*GQ. Wired. Rolling Stone.* Gran had them framed and on the wall in the library, until it happened. Then she took them down."

"I just bet she did," Jack said.

"I'm so sorry I put you through that," Maddie said. "I didn't know how bad it would be. I was just thinking about myself. Not what it would cost you."

"Do you understand now what I was trying to tell you last night?" he asked gently. "The price is real, Maddie."

"I don't accept it," she said, her voice rebellious.

Jack sighed. "Reality doesn't give a damn if you accept it or not."

"We'll clear your name," she said. "We'll prove it to everyone."

"What if we don't?" He stroked a springy, corkscrewing lock of her hair back off her forehead. "Or what if we prove it, but people still doubt us? I might be dragging this thing behind me my whole life. Just admit that the problem is a real one. That's all I ask."

She grabbed his hand. "Yes, it's real, but have

faith. I want you to believe that we can find a life that's good. Even if we have to go away. Europe, Asia, Australia."

"And what about your grandmother? She's old, Maddie."

"Please," she said. "One thing at a time. Just promise me you'll fight like hell."

He considered it for a moment, gazing at her amber-colored eyes, blazing with fierce intensity. Maddie was a golden child, like Caleb, capable of bending the world to her will. She thought she could do the same on his behalf. Just use her powers to make it all okay.

Who knew. Maybe she actually could. But it wouldn't happen unless he was all in.

Jack nodded slowly. "Okay," he said, "I'll fight like a demon from hell. For you."

"For us," she corrected.

He smiled at her, and lifted her hand to his lips. "For us," he agreed.

Fourteen

Maddie called downstairs to get them checked out. They changed into their normal clothes and melted away without engaging with anyone else from the wedding. Neither one of them felt like being social after those two disturbing encounters.

They were very quiet in the car as Jack drove them down the mountain highway.

"Hey," Jack said, after a long silence. "Thanks for sticking up for me, when Ronnie found us in the library."

She reached out, and squeezed his thigh. "They're all going to feel terrible when they find out how badly they misjudged you," she said. "And I, for one, will enjoy it."

Jack let out a dry laugh. "Nice little fantasy, but I outgrew it years ago."

"Try it on again," Maddie told him. "Things are about to change."

"Things already have changed," Jack said. "Just having you on my side changes everything. Everything feels different." They passed an exit sign, and he turned to her. "Do you want me to take you home? You'll have to give me some directions."

"No, not home. Marcus and Gran would show up for sure, and I just can't face it. Tomorrow I have that lunch date at the bistro, with Amelia Howard. You?"

"I have to do a bunch of prep work for Monday's meetings. I'm meeting with some potential manufacturing partners for the enzymatic recycling products we're developing. Shall we stop at a hotel, then?"

"Let's go to the Crown Royale. It's centrally located, and I know the general manager. MossTech keeps a suite there, so we're in and out of there all the time."

Jack glanced over at her, looking alarmed. "You aren't proposing staying in the MossTech suite, are you?"

"By no means," she assured him. "We'll have our own suite. Never fear."

She called the hotel, and set it all up. Penthouse suite. Panoramic terrace. Hot tub. King-size bed. By the time she'd finished, they were almost there, and Jack was laughing under his breath, shaking his head.

They left their car to be parked by the attendant and their luggage to be brought up to the room, and went in to the front desk to collect their keys.

He studied her intently in the elevator going up. At the door of the suite, Maddie held up the key to the sensor, and turned to him as soon as they were inside, the door closed behind them. "What's that look all about?" she demanded. "What have I done now?"

"I was just impressed," he said. "The magic phone calls that shift the axis of reality and re-stitch the fabric of space and time. One phone call from Maddie Moss, and the sun would rise in the west, if she so desired. It's your secret superpower."

"Superpower, ha," she scoffed. "I just happen to be in and out of this place a lot, so they know me. And I know the general manager. We dated for a while."

Jack's eyes sharpened. "Really? So what happened?"

"It didn't work out."

"No? Why not?"

She frowned at him. "It's not really your business, you know."

"Yes, I do know that," he admitted. "But I'm still curious."

She rolled her eyes. "I don't really like to say it because it sounds kind of mean," she told him. "But I got bored. There was no heat. We're just good friends. Still are."

"Ah." He thought about that for a moment. "So I don't bore you?"

She shook her head slowly back and forth. "Nope," she whispered. "You sure don't, Jack Daly."

That earned her one of those devastating grins. The delicious, crackling heat roared up between them.

In that moment, the porter came to the door with the luggage.

When he was tipped and gone, she watched Jack wander around the huge, luxurious room. He looked out at the big terrace, the skyline view, the bucket of ice with the bottle of Veuve Clicquot, the vase of floating, ethereal orchids.

He stroked an orchid petal with his fingertip. "Very nice," he said softly. "Orchids. Only the best for the Mosses."

His tone gave her pause. "I hope you don't resent me for that."

"Not at all," he said. "I might have been conflicted about it when I was younger. In high school. It seemed to me then as if Caleb and the rest of you lived like royalty."

"Caleb thought that the BioSpark thing happened because you were jealous," she said.

Jack looked horrified. "God, no. He was my best friend. And your family was so good to me. I was dazzled by the luxury, yes, but not jealous. And even less so, now."

"Less so?" That made her curious. "Why is that?"

Jack gazed intently at the orchid blossom. "We were living pretty large back then," he said slowly. "When things started picking up for Bio-Spark. There was a lot of money coming in, and more on the horizon. Sweet cars, sharp clothes, hot girlfriends. Apartments in two cities. I had my penthouse in San Francisco, and Gabriella found me a condo in Seattle, too. Caleb and I had plans for swanky corporate headquarters with a view of the Bay. Even a corporate jet. Then, one day, boom. It was all gone, and I was back down to zero. Below zero, actually. I would say that prison definitely puts you below."

Maddie reached out, putting her hand on his arm. "I'm so sorry, Jack."

"Don't be," he said. "I wasn't looking for pity. It was a long time ago, and I'm fine now. Even financially. It took a while, and it's not Moss levels, but I do okay."

"I didn't mean to open a can of worms," she said.

"You didn't," he assured her. "I'm trying to explain myself. When you get money and then you lose it, you start to understand deep in your bones that it's just a game. Smoke and mirrors. Ones and zeros on a screen. Whose dick is bigger. Now that I've seen through it, I can never take it seriously, ever again. It's lost its grip on me."

Maddie considered his words. "I think that may just be your secret superpower, Jack. Or one of them, at least."

He laughed out loud. "Oh, yeah? Really? How do you figure?"

"You might not see it that way, but most people are battling to the death in that stupid game. Not you. You're already free. You don't have to wait until your third divorce or your deathbed to figure it out, all full of regrets. You're there right now. Lucky you."

He laughed. "I never saw it quite that way, but a win is a win, I guess. And that said…" He gestured at the champagne chilling in the bucket. "Can I pour us a glass?"

"Yes, please. That would be great. I'm just going to change. Be right back."

In the bedroom, Maddie rummaged through her suitcase. She'd hit rock bottom when it came to fresh clothing, but her silk nightgown was clean. She tossed it over her head, and let the champagne-pink fabric settle around her, whispery soft. It had delicate spaghetti straps, lace insets, and it skimmed her curves, the skirt swaying above her ankles. She fluffed up her hair, brushed her teeth, slicked on lip gloss.

When she went back out, Jack was gazing out the window, silhouetted against the skyline. He turned to look at her, and his eyes went hot. "Oh, wow. Maddie."

Her face was very warm, but she brazened it out, smiling and twirling for him. "Do you like my sweet silky nothings? We skipped the sexy nightie part of the evening's festivities last night, so I thought we could make up for lost time tonight."

He shook his head. "I'm just...my God. I forget how to talk when I look at you."

"It appears to be just a momentary lapse," she observed. "In my experience, you recover quickly, and then you're capable of talking for hours."

"True enough." He turned toward the ice bucket. "Want that champagne now?"

"Lay it on me," she said. "God, what a day."

Jack expertly popped the cork, and poured out two flutes of the ice-cold, fizzy champagne, passing one to her. "To momentary lapses," he said.

She lifted her glass. "To secret superpowers."

They clinked glasses, laughing. The champagne was a sensual explosion. The burn of the fizz, the icy cold, the bright flavor. They savored it silently, and then Maddie moved closer to him, and linked her arm through his, lifting her glass.

"To trust," she said.

The look in his eyes shook her inside. They were suspended in an odd, timeless silence. Jack finally let out a slow breath, and lifted his own glass.

"To trust," he said, his voice uneven. "Thank you."

They drank, arms linked. The moment felt almost ceremonial.

Jack slid his arm around the small of her back. "I love that you trust me," he said, in a low, wondering voice. "I still can't quite believe it."

Maddie set down her champagne flute on the table, then took his and set it down, too. "I feel you, Jack." She patted her heart. "Inside. This part of me I never felt or knew before just knows you're for real. There's no way to fake that. It's in there, or it's not."

"I feel it, too," he said. "It scares me to death."

"Why? You're safe with me. Trust makes us safe."

Jack's gaze was stark. "Nothing makes us safe."

She put her hand against his cheek. "Nothing? Ever?"

He shook his head. "I've taught myself to let go of a lot of things. I take it all lightly now. Money, fame, ambition, my reputation, whatever. I've lightened my grip on all these things by sheer necessity. But I just can't do that with you."

Maddie reached up, looping her arms around his neck.

"Then don't," she said. "Hang on tight. Never let me go."

"God, no," he whispered, as their lips met.

Fifteen

Slow down. Cool it. Breathe, Daly.

He was teetering on the edge of reason, and the final blow was that sheer, silky nightgown that showed every detail of her body. He couldn't lift his hands away. Couldn't lighten up the desperate kisses. The jut of her dark nipples against his chest, his hands cupping, stroking the warm curves of her hips, it was driving him wild. He was a heartbeat away from screwing this up. Being too emotional. Out of control.

His hands were constantly amazed by the exquisite softness of her. The smooth, supple texture of her skin. The springy, luscious swell of her breasts. Every ticklish stroke a lick of fiery awareness. The fine fabric of her night-gown snagged on the rough parts of his hands. He gripped the curve of her waist, pulling her against the hot, aching bulge in his pants.

Maddie pressed closer, gasping with eagerness. Jack reached down, tugging up the nightgown, and slid his hand reverently up the silken heat of her thighs. So smooth. All the way up to the luscious curve of her...*oh...yes.*

No panties. Not one stitch. Just soft skin, silky fuzz and her slick, hot, secret woman flesh, wet and welcoming, yielding to his probing hand.

"Maddie," he moaned against her ear. "You're just...perfect. So hot."

"Touch me there, while you kiss me," she directed. "I love the way you do it."

He couldn't even speak, but she felt his passionate assent.

He was swept into an altered state of consciousness by her luscious mouth, by the sinuous moving of her lithe, vibrant body against his hand. He sought out her tongue with his own, delving in as he probed that hot well of slick moisture, caressing that tight nub of exquisite sensation between her legs, coaxing her right toward where she needed to go, following her shivers, her breathless moans.

She arched back, rigid, crying out as her climax pulsed through her body.

When her eyes fluttered open, their gazes locked, and it was time.

There was a brief, confusing tussle of wrenching the bedcovers off, then his shoes, his belt buckle, his buttons, his socks. They worked together to strip it all off like the fate of the world depended on it. At last, he was naked, and Maddie was stretched out on the rumpled sheets, her arms lifted up to him. The silk nightie pooled up around her waist, showing everything, the thin shoulder straps fallen down so that her nipples peeked over the scalloped lace of her neckline.

He was helpless. He would do anything to satisfy her. He'd resolved, in the last rational part of his mind that was still active, to keep it slow, make sure he made her come again, but there was no way to slow this down now, not with her dragging him down on top of her, her strong legs twining around his waist, her nails digging into him. Egging him on.

He eased himself inside her hot depths. So tight, hugging him, but so slick and welcoming. Her perfect body clung, caressing him with each deep stroke.

There was a lot of noise, and he was making

some of it himself. The big, heavy bed vibrated against the floor, and pleasure kept swelling, bigger every time until it encompassed everything, and they came together, explosively.

They lay there for a sweet forever. First panting and sweat-dampened. Then floating and dreamy. Finally, Maddie stirred, yawning, and gave him a smile that set off fresh fireworks, deep in his body. She was so pretty. He just couldn't get used to it.

"Wow," she whispered. "That was amazing. Like it always is."

"Yeah." Jack coughed, clearing his throat. Raspy from the gasping, the shouting. "Every time, it gets more intense. I don't understand the math of that. How it can just keep getting better. I mean, where can it possibly go from here?"

She propped herself up onto her elbow, giving him a very direct look. "Home," she said. "It goes home. To your friends, to your job, to your rightful place in the world."

Jack wound his fingers through her curls. "It's not your job to solve my life, much as I love you for wanting to," he reminded her. "We can only do that for ourselves."

"I know that," she said. "But I still want to help."

"You already have," he told her. "What you've done is a miracle. Your trust, your understanding. Yourself. I'm so lucky. Even if this was all I got, I'd feel lucky."

"Well, it's not all," she said. "So don't think that."

He pulled her closer. "I'm just trying to be grateful. To stay in the moment."

"The moment is great," Maddie said sternly. "Tomorrow will be great, too."

"I don't trust tomorrow. But I do trust you."

Maddie smacked his chest. "Oh, stop it. You're going all Zen-dude on me. Come back down to earth."

"Oh, I'm with you." He seized her hand and slid it down, to feel the stiff heat of his erection, stubbornly high and hard against his belly. "And feeling pretty damn earthy."

At that moment, his stomach rumbled, and Maddie's beautiful lips curved in amusement. "Speaking of earthy. Let's order up some food before we get involved again. They have an excellent chef here. The room service menu is legendary."

"Sounds great to me," he said.

Maddie sat up, and grabbed the phone by the bed. "Yes, this is Maddie Moss, in the east penthouse suite," she said. "I'd like to order dinner to be sent up... Yes. We'll have the Chef's Choice for two... No, we want to be surprised... Oh, yes, definitely include a couple of desserts... Red wine, yes, unless it's mostly fish... Sure, whatever Gianfranco recommends. Thanks." She hung up. "It's a mystery meal, but rest assured, it'll be good."

"Whatever Gianfranco recommends? Whoohoo. Look out, Maddie. You're showing your secret superpower again."

"Nah. You've mistaken it for my credit card."

That led to a playful, giggling tussle on the bed that ended with Maddie straddling him and moving over him in a way that drove him mad. Looking down on him with those hot, sultry, heavy-lidded eyes that just made him throb with need.

But she shook her head in answer to the silent question in his eyes. "They'll be here with the food pretty soon," she said breathlessly. "We'll get back to this after. Definitely. Let me get you some more champagne. And I'm grabbing a quick shower."

Jack threw on the terry cloth robe the hotel had provided, and refilled their champagne flutes while she was in the shower. Jack felt euphoric.

Flying higher than he'd ever been in his life. Buzzed on champagne, and Maddie.

The knock sounded on the door. "Room service," a voice called.

"I've got the door," he called to Maddie, who had just emerged, fragrant and damp and perfumed, wrapped in her own robe.

The waiter pushed in a rolling tray crowded with covered dishes, and went away grinning hugely. True love and wild sex had made Jack an extremely generous tipper.

The food was amazing. It consisted of multiple plates of finger food. Fried eggplant wrapped around aged caciocavallo cheese, bubbling in tomato sauce. Mint-scented zucchini fritters. Calabrese friselle, loaded with oil, basil, creamy stracciatella cheese and glowing golden datterino tomatoes. Meltingly tender oven-roasted pork roll-ups, crackling in an earthenware terrine. Fresh tagliatelle pasta with cream and black truffle. Tender crepes filled with sheep's milk ricotta and wild mushrooms. A cheese plate, a fruit platter. A lemon cream cake, a plate of fudgy brownies and chocolate-dipped shortbreads for dessert.

Every bite was amazing, but nothing had ever tasted so good as Maddie's kiss.

They feasted, laughing and talking. Then, at

one point, all the words just drained away, and were replaced by that buzzing heat that he'd begun to crave.

Maddie stood up, took his hand and tugged. He let her lead him back to the bedroom, then pushed her down until she sat on the bed, and knelt in front of her, stroking her bare knees as the terry cloth robe fell open over her thighs, then over her belly. Then her breasts. He pulled the sash free, and stroked down her knees in silent pleading, until her legs fell open, and he leaned forward, pressing his face to her sweet, tender folds. Taking his time. Caressing them worshipfully with his lips, his tongue. Lapping up her essence.

She stiffened, gasping, pressing herself to his face as pleasure rippled through her.

After the sweet tremors finally subsided, she rolled over and got up onto her knees, turning her back to him. Parted her thighs as she leaned forward on all fours. Lifted herself. "Like this," she invited him, her voice throaty. "Come here. Behind me."

"Oh, yeah."

Once again, he was too far out on the ledge to control the timing. Not with her on her knees, back arched, clutching the pillow. He gripped her hips, each heavy thrust jolting a shocked whimper from her throat. He saw them reflected in the picture window: her eyes were closed, gleaming lips parted, breasts swaying. Wailing in helpless pleasure as they pounded toward the explosive finish. He let go, losing himself inside her.

Such a perfect place to be lost. He never wanted to be found.

Sixteen

Maddie took a detour and drove past the lavish, space-age Energen facility on her way to the lunch meeting with Amelia.

It was impressive, completed only a few years ago by a prominent New York architecture firm. It was showy, a bold, innovative modern design, and it looked more like a docked spaceship than anything else. Lots of gleaming steel struts and unexpected angles, every part filled with glass, flooded with light.

She couldn't help but reflect, as she circled the enormous complex, that the outrageous price tag of this building had been paid with profits that had been stolen from Caleb and Jack.

But it was only money, and it was in the past now. Caleb and Jack were tough and smart, and there was more where that came from. When it came to ideas and innovation, those men would never need to steal from anyone.

If only she could just prove that, for Jack. Beyond the shadow of a doubt.

She drove to the bistro, left her car in a nearby garage and walked in. The place was buzzing with activity. The Sunday brunch crowd.

Amelia was already waiting for her, and stood up to shake her hand. She seemed sweet, but rather wispy and ethereal. She was a tall, pretty, dark-haired girl, with big, dreamy eyes, and she was clearly nervous.

They ordered a couple of chicken Caesar salads, and Maddie got right to work. She carefully and methodically asked Amelia about the most salient pieces of data that Jack had shown her, listening carefully for discrepancies. Most specifically, she concentrated on the research and development timelines of the Energen Vortex project.

Amelia's voice was hushed and tremulous, but she was very forthcoming, and she said nothing that was incongruent with what Jack had told her. After an hour or so of patient grilling,

Maddie was convinced that Amelia knew her stuff, and was telling her the simple truth. She also couldn't help but sense that this truth made the other woman feel sad, conflicted and guilty.

After she finished all of the questions that she'd prepared in her notes, she hesitated for a moment. "Amelia, may I ask you a personal question?"

"Um, okay," Amelia said, blinking rapidly.

"This whole thing seems to have made you extremely miserable," Maddie said.

"Oh, God, yes. It did, it really did. Jack didn't deserve any of that. He's the nicest guy. A true friend to me. And he was innocent of everything they said he did. Completely innocent."

"And yet, you didn't come out with this at the time."

Amelia's eyes slid away. "No," she murmured. "I didn't."

"Admittedly, you would've paid a very high price for doing so. But forgive me if I say that it looks to me like you're paying a pretty high price for it anyway."

"The truth is, when it all exploded, I'd just been checked into a private clinic," Amelia confessed. "I had a nervous breakdown, you see. And I was in there for a long time, heavily medicated. When I came out, Jack was in jail, and had been for months. I wanted to say something then, but when I visited Jack in prison, he urged me not to. He was afraid I'd have another break-down. He wanted to protect me. That's...that's just the kind of guy he is."

"Were you two together?" she asked.

"Oh, no," Amelia said swiftly. "Much as I would have loved to be. But he was with Gabri-ella at the time. No one would ever even dare to try and steal Gabriella's boyfriend. Gabriella's the type that would gladly wreck your life just for spite. Besides, I was involved with someone else back then. Which was why I had the ner-vous breakdown."

Maddie's curiosity was piqued, but Amelia grabbed her napkin and dabbed at her lips, her panicked gaze rising to whoever stood behind Maddie's chair.

"Hello, Amelia." It was a female voice, with a clear ring of accusation.

Amelia looked trapped. Maddie looked around.

A man and a woman stood there. The man was huge, with icy eyes and a lantern jaw, and his big, wide body looked like it had been shoe-horned into a business suit. The woman was a thin blonde with a taut, sharp jawline, dressed in a tight red minidress and red stiletto heels. Her lips were very red, and her eyebrows so dark, it was clear that the glossy blond ringlets had gotten chemical help.

"Hi, Gabriella," Amelia said, in a subdued voice. "What are you doing here?"

"Bill and I just happened to see you here," the woman said crisply. "So we came over to say hi. Who's your friend?"

"This is, ah... Maddie Moss," Amelia admitted, after a reluctant pause.

"Oh, really?" Gabriella's red lips twisted. "And what brings you here, Maddie?"

"I was in the neighborhood, so I took the opportunity to grab lunch with Amelia," Maddie said coolly.

"Really. I had no idea you two knew each other."

"How on earth would you?" Maddie asked. "I don't believe we've ever met. And your name is...?"

Amelia pulled herself together, with visible effort. "Maddie, this is Gabriella, our new senior VP of marketing, as of this Wednesday." She gestured behind her at the beefy guy without looking at him. "And that's Bill Greer, Energen's chief security officer."

Maddie offered her hand to each of them. "How do you do."

Bill Greer's hand was huge, sweaty and hot. It closed over hers in a strangling grip that stopped just short of pain. Gabriella's felt tense, as if her cold, thin hand were made out of twisted piano wire in a clammy glove. After the handshakes, they fixed Maddie with a cold stare, as if waiting for more information. To which they felt completely entitled.

When she offered none, Gabriella's eyes narrowed to slits. "Humph. Well, fine, then. Enjoy your lunch. Amelia, come see me tomorrow, when you get in to work. First thing. We definitely need to talk."

Gabriella gave them a fluttery finger wave and stalked away, heels clicking. Greer followed, shooting a cold, suspicious glare at her over his enormous shoulder.

When they were a safe distance, Maddie whistled. "Wow," she murmured. "That was weird."

"Yes, it was," Amelia said miserably. "Looks like I'm in for it. I wonder if they've been following me. Surveilling me."

Maddie was horrified. "Good God, Amelia. Do you really think they would?"

Amelia shrugged. "Since Gabriella got hired

a few days ago, yes, I do," she said. "She's been very cold to me since she got here. I think my days at Energen are numbered."

"I am so sorry if I made problems for you," Maddie said. "I guess we should have been even more discreet."

"It's okay," Amelia said quietly. "Maybe it's time to grit my teeth and face up to this, no matter what happens."

Maddie crossed her fingers, silently wishing the woman luck. "Tell me about those two," she asked.

"The nightmare pair," Amelia muttered. "Gabriella just showed up last week, like I said. She's clearly our CEO's new pet. And I can't believe she actually came to work here, after what happened with Jack."

Maddie gasped at the sudden realization. "Oh, my God! You mean, she's *that* Gabriella? Jack's ex? And she's working here now, at Energen? That is really strange."

"Agreed," Amelia said grimly. "And Greer? He's the guy I was going out with at the time. I hate him so hard. That snake. Ice in his chest instead of a heart."

"How did you meet him?" Maddie asked.

"At the condo complex. He was head of security there, at the time. That's where I met Gabriella. Then she finagled a condo one unit down and one unit over for Jack. I was 518, and he was 416. Jack and Gabriella were together back then. Engaged, I think."

"And you were with Greer," Maddie prompted.

"Yeah, Bill and I had this on again, off again affair. Sometimes he acted so sweet, and then suddenly he'd be ice-cold and bored with me. But I never knew how it would be. It made me frantic. I figured maybe it was because of his military background, you know? He was a Special Forces vet, and he saw a lot of combat, and that changes a guy. That's what I told myself, anyway."

"Then what happened? If you don't mind me asking," Maddie said cautiously. The woman seemed so brittle. The slightest breeze, and she'd shatter like fine crystal.

"It was that awful last night, in my apartment," Amelia said. "Bill had been acting strange again. He'd brought a bottle of wine, and he was all lovey-dovey during dinner, and then I got really faint. I must have passed out, because I woke up in the morning with the worst headache of my life, and Bill was gone. So I took some aspirin and went to work. And that morning, he came to my office. He told me loudly he was dumping me because I was a sloppy drunk, and it disgusted him. I tried to explain that I'd been sick, not drunk, but he didn't listen. He just left. And I... I crumbled. Jack was the one to come and get me. He gave me a ride home. And the next morning, I checked into the clinic."

Maddie put her hand out, and squeezed Amelia's hand. It was clammy and cold.

"What a cruel, horrible thing to do to you," she said fiercely. "And at your workplace, too. You mean, you have to see this asshole, every single working day?"

"I avoid him as much as possible," Amelia said. "But it looks like he and Gabriella are...together now. They deserve each other."

It was clearly painful for Amelia to dredge up her past heartbreaks to a stranger, so Maddie wrapped up the conversation, hoping against hope that she hadn't put Amelia in a bad spot with her employers. They said their goodbyes, and Amelia hurried away, clearly relieved that the conversation was over.

Maddie had a lot to think about as she made her way back to the parking garage. She had just pulled out her phone and was about to call

Jack and tell him what she'd experienced as she turned the corner to where she'd left her car.

She let out a cry, jerking back.

Gabriella Adriani and Bill Greer stood in front of her car. Staring at her like ghouls.

She blew out a sharp breath. "Good God! You guys startled me!"

"Sorry," Gabriella said, sounding anything but.

Maddie waited for them to move out of her way, but they just stood there, examining her as if she were an unexplained growth in a petri dish.

"Excuse me, but can I help you folks with something?" Maddie asked.

"I doubt it," Gabriella said. "But maybe we can help you."

"I didn't ask for help," Maddie said.

"I heard rumors that you were engaged to Jack Daly," Gabriella said.

"So?" Maddie said. "It's hardly your business."

"You might want to rethink that." Bill Greer's voice was oddly nasal and thin for such a big man, as if his sinuses were pinched closed.

"I didn't ask for your advice," Maddie said.

"We're not your enemy, Ms. Moss." Gabriella's voice was sweetly patronizing. "I understand the trap you've fallen into better than most. I got out just in time. Don't marry him. He can seem like the most honest guy you ever met, but he is a born predator."

Maddie clenched her arms around her purse, resisting the urge to back away. She had to stand her ground. Besides, that was her car behind them. "Thank you for sharing," she said. "Now get out of my way."

"What has he told you?" Greer took a step closer to her.

Maddie stepped back. "None of your business. Move, please."

"Come get a drink with us," Gabrielle coaxed. "We just want to talk to you."

"Not interested," Maddie said.

"We have information that you need," Gabriella pressed her. "You'll be glad you did."

Like hell. "Move," she repeated, icily.

"At least, take this." Greer held out a small object. A flash drive, she realized.

Maddie shrank away from it. "What the hell is that?"

"The truth about Jack Daly," Greer said. "I was head of security at his condominium complex. This is video of the night he invested seven hundred thousand dollars in Energen stock, the day before their public offering. I have video of his door, the lobby and two shots of the outside building. The only person going in and out is him and Gabriella, and she left the apartment an hour and a half before the order was placed. She was out of the building altogether. But don't take it from me. Watch the tape. It speaks for itself. The only person who could have possibly placed that order was Daly himself."

Gabriella let out a martyred sigh. "I was such an idiot, believing in him."

"You were there that night?" Maddie asked.

"I was the last one out of the apartment," Gabriella said. "He was drunk, and he was getting ugly, so I went home at 12:22. As you will see on the tape, if you have the guts to look at it. That was the night he bought the Energen stock. He'd lost faith in his own product. He knew that Carbon Clean was fatally flawed, and he wanted to cash out as much as possible before anyone found out. The Energen product was a better design, and he knew it. And when word got out, sure enough, BioSpark's IPO tanked. But the message was traced back to Jack's IP address. His desktop computer, in his apartment. He got sloppy and didn't mask it. Probably because he was drunk. Not thinking clearly. I remember it well. I was so upset that night, I went out to meet some girlfriends for a drink afterwards."

"Bullshit," Maddie said.

"Honey, face it." Gabriella's voice was pitying. "Jack Daly is guilty as sin, and if he tells you otherwise, he's lying." Her lips twisted, the lipstick garish against her skin.

"Stop harassing me, or I'm calling the cops," Maddie said.

Gabriella and Greer glanced at each other. Greer leaned over, and dropped the flash drive into the outside pocket of Maddie's purse. "Look at the video," he said again. "It speaks for itself."

"They all say you're supposed to be so smart," Gabriella said. "Show it."

Maddie pushed past them, and got into her car. They stepped out of her way as she revved the engine, and in the rearview mirror, she saw them staring after her as she turned the corner.

Her phone began to ring. She was too rattled to answer it. She pawed at her purse, glanced at the phone. It was Jack's name on the display.

Oh, God. Not now.

That encounter had completely unnerved her. She was shaking. Her purse lay open on the seat, and the flash drive had fallen out. Just a simple plastic rectangle, but it looked malevolent. As if it were radioactive.

Maddie drove aimlessly, trying to make her mind stop racing. She'd gone to Energen to fish for some more info, and instead, she'd been blasted with more than she could swallow. Jack called again, twice more, but she didn't pull over to answer.

Eventually she found herself in her own neighborhood. She pulled off on a side street, still not ready to put weight on her shaky legs. She fished out her laptop, and hesitated for only a moment before plugging in the drive.

After all, Gabriella and Greer were in no position to make accusations, given that they were both working for Energen now. Amelia had said that Gabriella was the CEO's pet. She and Greer were lovers. They'd all lived on top of each other at the condo complex where Greer did security. It stank. Whatever she found on that flash drive, she'd take with a whole handful of salt, not just a grain.

She opened the video, and set the four displays to play simultaneously, two indoor, and the two outdoor, of Building 6 of the Sylvan Luxury Condominiums. The time frame covered eight hours, starting at 8:00 p.m.

Even fast-forwarding, Maddie had never stared so intently at something so boring for so long. She sat there for what felt like forever, watching numbers flash on the bar showing the passage of time, while absolutely nothing happened on the screen. She slowed down, checking every flash of movement on the screen, when someone walked in or out.

At the eight o'clock mark, she slowed down a flash of movement, and spotted Jack walking in the front door of the building and heading toward the elevator. Moments later, she saw him exit the elevator on the fourth floor, unlock his door, and go inside.

At 9:23, Gabriella came to the door, knocked and walked in, and another long, dull bout of nothing-to-see-here began. Gabriella walked back out of the apartment at 12:22 a.m., looking agitated. She slammed the door and stalked toward the elevator, anger radiating from her thin, narrow shoulders. Fifteen minutes later, she emerged from the elevator in the lobby, and left the building.

Then, once again, nothing. She slowed down the film and watched the critical period between 1:30 a.m. and 2:30 a.m. in real time, when the fateful order to the stockbroker had been sent.

Only Jack was in that apartment. Only Jack could have used that computer, with that IP address. His encryption had made hacking and spoofing an impossibility. He'd said so himself.

Outside the building, she saw nothing. He had two balconies leading to the bedroom and the living area. Both of them had closed doors and showed no movement, though lights were on inside. The only movement was the wind moving the leaves of the big tree outside the building. The sway of the branches.

She ran the video back, over and over. Baffled. No one had gone in. No one had gone out. She could see that from every angle, every entrance.

The truth is staring you right in the face.

Caleb had gone through this agonizing process, too. He'd been unable to believe that Jack was capable of doing this…but the evidence was overwhelming. The encryption on the desktop computer. The order to buy the stock, from that IP address. The plane ticket. The offshore bank account. The money deposited in it.

Still, Jack had no motive to do what they had accused him of doing. Unless, of course, he was different than she had perceived him. She wouldn't be the first to misjudge a man she'd fallen in love with.

She just couldn't make this square with her powers of reason. If it were true, then Jack was broken inside. A liar who was drawing her into a trap. Using her to hurt Caleb. Making a fool of her.

No. It wasn't possible. She couldn't believe it—but she couldn't un-see the blatant evidence against him, either. It was squeezing her mind like a vise.

She could hardly breathe from the pressure.

She snapped the laptop shut, and drove home. She pulled her suitcase out of the car, with the vague intention of dumping out dirty clothes, and loading up with fresh ones.

Her home seemed strangely unfamiliar when she walked inside. The Maddie Moss who had lived here a week ago was a different woman, inhabiting a different world.

She'd been trained, as a scientist and as a person, to follow truth the way a sailor followed the North Star, but truth had never flat out betrayed her like this before.

She pulled out some clothes, at random. Some work stuff, some casual stuff. She was usually meticulous about planning outfits when traveling. Mixing and matching so that every piece could serve double or triple duty. Tonight, she couldn't focus at all.

She changed out of the suit she wore, and threw on some soft ripped jeans, and a long, slate-blue sweater made of loose-knit raw silk. She splashed her face in the sink. Swabbed off her raccoon smudges. Mascara and emotional turmoil did not mix.

She looked around, wondering what she was forgetting, but whatever. She could always come back later. She tossed on a leather jacket, and opened the front door.

Her entire family was arrayed on the lawn, right in front of her porch.

Oh, God. There was Caleb, back early from Spain, looking like she'd just stabbed him right through the heart. Tilda, his beautiful blonde bride, was next to him. Those two lovebirds were blissfully happy together, and were usually laughing and whispering into each other's ears, but they weren't smiling now.

Her second brother, Marcus, was back from one of his many trips to Asia. Like Caleb, Marcus looked nothing like her, taking after his mystery father. His genetic test had revealed Japanese and Korean ancestry, but the only sure thing about the guy was that he must have been tall and good-looking, because Marcus was starkly handsome. His thick black hair had gotten very long, and he had sharp cheekbones, a chiseled jaw, keen dark eyes.

Gran was in the middle, standing bolt upright, as perfectly dressed as ever, her snow-white spiky pixie cut perfectly styled. But she looked stricken. And scared.

Seeing Gran look scared was unnerving in the extreme.

The suitcase fell from Maddie's hand, thudding on the porch by her feet.

"Hey," she said. "What's this about? Is my house under surveillance?"

No one replied, for a long moment, and then Gran spoke up. "Not exactly, love. Can we come in? I'd prefer not to have this conversation with your neighbors watching."

"Just tell me," Maddie asked. "Did you guys stake out my place? Because I am not okay with that. It's creepy and controlling, and I won't stand for it."

"We'll discuss that issue inside as well," Gran said.

The regal authority in Gran's tone worked its usual magic, and Maddie stepped aside, letting them all file past into her house. She hoped when she was in her eighties that she would possess that handy superpower. One could only hope.

"Make us coffee, sweetheart," Gran admonished. "Did you forget your manners?"

"I'm not the one who's spying and sneaking and bursting in uninvited. I don't think anyone here has the right to lecture me about manners," Maddie said.

"Even so. Coffee, please."

Oh, what the hell. She got to work in her kitchen, setting up the coffee maker and scooping in grounds.

Tilda joined her in the kitchen, pulling down coffee mugs from the cupboard, and setting them on the table. She leaned close, and kissed Maddie's cheek. "Don't be upset," she whispered. "We all love you. You know that. Nobody is going to attack you."

Maddie gave Tilda a sidewise look. "Thanks, sweetie. Maybe you won't, but you'd better not speak for them."

When all the coffee had hissed and gurgled down into the pot, she set it out on the table near the mugs and the fixings, and briskly brushed off her hands.

"There. My sacred hostess duty is now done," she said. "Please, help yourself to coffee. Now, maybe you could just tell me. To what do I owe the honor of this visit?"

Caleb and Marcus exchanged grim glances.

"Don't play dumb, Maddie," Caleb said.

"At first, we were all furious," Gran broke in, pouring out coffee for everyone. "Then Ronnie told us about Ava's wedding. What you said to her there. And we realized that the problem was much bigger than we'd ever dreamed."

"Spare me the dramatic language, please," Maddie muttered.

Gran reached out and put her hand on Maddie's. "Tell me the truth, sweetheart. Are you in love with him? Ronnie was convinced that you were. I hope it isn't true."

Maddie opened and closed her mouth. Her emotions were too tender and raw to throw out in front of her family when they were in this mood. Or ever, really.

"My feelings are my own private business, Gran," she said stiffly. "What's relevant here is that I have reason to believe that Jack is innocent."

Marcus put his coffee down so sharply, coffee slopped out onto the table. "Damn. Here we go. Strap in for the roller coaster ride of objective reality, Mads."

"Marcus, do not start," Maddie said.

"We have to." Caleb's voice was hard. "Because we love you."

"I have very compelling evidence," Maddie said. "All I ask is for you to look at the big picture one last time. To have an open mind."

"I'm not opening a damn thing to that bastard. He stabbed me in the back. He waited until the perfect moment to do the greatest possible damage to BioSpark, and to me personally. Now, years later, he sees you, and sees a fresh and entertaining way to hurt me again, by hurting you. I can't let him do it, Mads."

"But it's not like that, Caleb," Maddie pleaded. "He was set up."

"He was not." Caleb slammed a huge manila accordion file down on the table. "I'm not supposed to have this, and Detective Stedman would be furious, but I called in some favors at the police department and had Jack's file copied. I went through it myself, and flagged the important parts for you. Things that would be impossible to fake."

"There's no sign of intrusion at his apartment, Mads," Marcus said. "And the trade in Energen stock came from there. No fingerprints but his, Gabriella's and the people from the cleaning service. The ticket to Rio has his fingerprints all over the envelope. And the email to that broker was from his IP address."

"Either he sold our research data to Energen, or he decided that theirs was better than ours, and threw us under the bus," Caleb said. "I'm not sure which is worse. But the police file has multiple clips of him visiting Energen in the months previously, from Energen's security footage. Unexplained visits."

"He was good friends with a woman who worked there," Maddie argued. "Amelia Howard was her name. He visited her sometimes. And speaking of Energen, you guys don't think it's strange that Gabriella is suddenly working there now, after everything that happened?"

Caleb shrugged. "I never liked the woman, but she wasn't in that apartment when that order was placed, Maddie. It wasn't her. Maybe Energen is the best she can do now. Poor her."

Maddie shook her head. "You don't have the guts to give Jack an instant's chance, even in your own head. You won't consider that he might have been set up. That's unfair."

"Very," Caleb said. "I'm sure that was the problem all along, from back when we were in high school together, and college. I had no problems paying for school, or taking internships, or having a nice apartment. I'm sure he thought that was very unfair."

"He's not like that! Just give him a break!"

"Baby, we can't," Gran said gently. "That door is closed. It has to be."

"I'm sorry that you're in love with him, Maddie," Caleb said. "But switch on your brain and grow up, for God's sake."

Gran squeezed Maddie's fingers. "My poor love," she said gently. "I hate that this ugliness had to touch you. I would have done anything to spare you. I'm so sorry."

"Me, too." Tilda squeezed her shoulder. Her big green eyes were wet. "Annika is still at Gran's place, and she would love to see you. Would you come back with us? So we can all be together?"

"No." Maddie's voice was choked. "Please, all of you. Just go away. I know you mean well, but I need to be alone."

Gran got up, drawing herself up to her full height, and Maddie braced herself, knowing the look on her grandmother's face all too well.

"Whatever you meant to accomplish by this idiocy, the mandate still stands," Gran announced. "Remember this, sweetheart. I will always love you. To the moon and back. Never forget it. But if you choose that man, don't come to my home. Don't call me. Don't write me. If you choose him, you must cut off all contact with me. It breaks my heart, but those are the consequences of your actions."

Maddie swallowed over the rock-hard lump in her throat. She looked at her brothers. "How about you guys? Am I dead to you, too?"

Caleb looked miserable. "I don't want that man around my wife and kid, any more than I want him around my sister."

"Please, Mads," Marcus said tightly. "Don't do this to us."

Tilda put her hand on Maddie's arm. "Honey—"

"I get it," she said, flinching away. "I understand. If I do this, I'm on my own. Forevermore. Just leave, please. So I can contemplate that in peace."

Her family filed out the door, and Maddie shut the door behind them. She peeked through the blinds until they were in their cars and had driven away. Tilda with Caleb, Gran with Marcus.

Gone. All of them. For good, maybe. If she threw in her lot with Jack. Oh, God.

She stumbled back into her kitchen and sank

heavily down on a chair, staring down at the jumbled cups, the coffee rings, the spilled sugar.

And that huge, forbidding file. Challenging her faith with its weight and size.

She put out a reluctant hand and pulled it toward herself. She slid out the heavy, jumbled sheaf of paper, and began to read.

Seventeen

Jack pulled the sedan he'd just rented into the parking garage of the Crowne Suites, and got out his phone. For the umpteenth time. He reminded himself to breathe.

Earlier that afternoon, after her lunch with Amelia, Maddie had gone suddenly incommunicado. No more calls, no more text messages. It didn't seem in character for her, but of course, today was the first day since Paradise Point that they'd been apart. Maybe she liked her privacy and resented being constantly badgered. Some hyperconcentrated types were like that. Hell, he'd been like that himself, back in the day, when working on a project that consumed him. He could forget the rest of the world existed. Maybe he was just being needy.

Yeah. Keep telling yourself that, Daly. A woman in love didn't act that way.

He tried calling her again, but it went straight to voice mail. He didn't bother leaving another message. He'd left more than one already.

Damn. It wasn't as if he could call her family to make sure she was okay.

His own day had gone fine, until Maddie cut off communication. He'd gotten everything organized for tomorrow's meetings with the potential manufacturing partners for the enzymatic recycling products he'd helped develop, and then he'd gone out to rent himself a car. It looked like his efforts to rehabilitate his life and win back some semblance of his chosen career were bearing fruit.

That called for another bottle of champagne and another fabulous Chef's Choice meal with Maddie. Maybe even a long soak in a hot tub out on the terrace, looking over the glittering skyline. Naked in steaming hot bubbling water, with the most beautiful woman in the world.

A woman who wouldn't return his calls.

When he walked into the penthouse suite, it was dark and empty. Not that he'd been expecting her, but his heart still somehow managed to thud down a few more stories.

He stared out the window at the sparkling skyline. He remembered how he'd perceived the city lights as a very young man, clueless and innocent, everything still ahead of him. Those lights were possibilities, mysteries to solve. The city had been his to conquer. Then things had gone bad, and the lights had seemed like a million glittering, accusing eyes.

Then he'd gone to prison. No bright lights in that place. Just darkness.

Maddie's suitcase was gone. No sign of her at all. Last night had been so full of hope and possibility. Now, in the silence, all he felt was a sinking sense of dread.

Jack stripped off the suit and tie, threw on some jeans and a sweatshirt, and headed down to the bar with his phone in his hand, just in case Maddie called. He proceeded to prowl through the huge lobby, conference rooms, coffee shops, both of the cafés, the restaurant, looking for her. Then the gym, the spa. Back to the bar.

And there she was. She must have come in while he was cruising the rest of the place. She sat at the end of the bar, her face reflected in the mirror between shelves of liquor. She wore jeans and a loose blue sweater, her hair a wild cloud of ringlets.

Her eyes were down. She had a drink in front of her. A tumbler of whiskey.

When he approached, she saw him, and lifted her glass to him, unsmiling. "Hey."

Jack stopped a few steps away, chilled. "You turned off your phone."

"I really needed to concentrate today," she told him.

That made him irrationally angry. "Really? For nine hours?"

"Yes." She offered no further explanation.

Jack looked down at her drink. "What's with that? I've never seen you drink whiskey. I thought you liked mojitos, cosmopolitans, Moscow mules, margaritas."

"They seemed too frivolous tonight." Her tone seemed distant. "Not right for my mood. I needed something serious. This is what Gran drinks when she's upset with us. Fine, single malt Oban Scotch, aged for fourteen years. A grown-up's drink."

Ah. So there would be no celebrating tonight. Jack caught the eye of the bartender and pointed at Maddie's drink. "I'll have what she's having," he said.

The woman glanced at his face, and sloshed a very generous shot into the tumbler. Taking pity on him. He could see his own face reflected in the mirrored wall, and he knew that grim look. Braced for pain.

Jack sat down next to Maddie and took a sip. The whiskey went down with a deep, earthy burn. It tasted like fire and smoke.

Time to get this over with. "So tell me about your day," he said.

Maddie rubbed her eyes. She wore no makeup, and her face looked soft and vulnerable. "Well, I had a very interesting conversation with Amelia," she began. "She struck me as a sad and fragile person who badly needs to find a new job. That place is toxic for her. But she corroborated everything you showed me, very authoritatively. Much good it does you, if she doesn't have the guts to stand up for you."

"She was already checked into the clinic when the hammer fell on me," he said. "She was sick. And when she finally got out of that place, I was already in prison. Then, when I got out, I figured, why destroy her life, too? They could have really hurt her."

Maddie grunted under her breath. "Then Gabriella Adriani and Bill Greer ran into us at the bistro. What are the odds? She's their new senior VP, evidently. Just hired."

"Gabriella's working at Energen?" Jack was genuinely startled by this news.

"Yes. And Bill Greer, too, as chief security officer. According to Amelia, Bill and Gabriella are lovers."

Jack made a face. "That must really suck for Amelia. Are you sure that it's the same woman?"

"As sure as sure can be," Maddie said.

"So?" Jack prompted. "Then what happened?"

Maddie shrugged. "Not much, at first. They did a little intimidation routine with Amelia, and made her miserable, but I got the sense that's nothing unusual. But then Gabriella and Greer followed me into the parking garage, and cornered me."

Chills raced up Jack's spine. He put the whiskey glass down. "They did *what*?"

"You heard me. Greer gave me a flash drive with the security footage from that night at the Sylvan Luxury Condos, when the email was sent to the broker."

"I see," he said. "Did you watch it?"

"I did," she admitted.

Jack looked down into his whiskey glass. "I

cannot account for that tape," he said, his voice bleak. "I just cannot understand it."

"I know," Maddie whispered. "I know."

They stared straight ahead for a moment as they sipped their whiskey.

"Was that why you turned off your phone?" Jack finally asked.

"Partly," Maddie said. "After that, I went home to fill my suitcase with fresh clothes, and Gran and Caleb and Marcus and Tilda all descended on me. Evidently, they had staked out my house. It's just that kind of day."

Jack gestured to the bartender for another shot. "So you're saying that they got to you?"

"Not exactly. Caleb brought a photocopy of Detective Stedman's file. He left it for me to look through."

"I see," Jack said, his voice colorless.

"It's not that they got to me," Maddie said. "It's just a lot to take in. It's a huge file. It looks bad."

True. That file had blown his mind, too. Everything in it was both completely fabricated, and somehow, completely airtight. As if he'd been placed under some evil spell. That goddamn IP address on his desktop, damning him to hell.

"You're right about that," he admitted. "I know it looks bad."

"It's just so crazy," she said. "The email to the broker from your IP address, the security tapes that show no one went inside after Gabriella left, her taking off for the nightclub, the plane ticket with your fingerprints on the envelope, the fake IDs, the investments in Panama—"

"Maddie," he repeated, though he knew it was useless. "I told you about this stuff before. I told you that it wasn't me. Even though it looks like it was."

She turned her beautiful, intense, golden eyes on his face, studying him like she was trying to see right into his soul. "Jack, I…" Her voice trailed off. She waved her hands expressively. "It's not that I don't believe you. And it's not that I don't love you. I'm just…so confused. It's tearing me apart. You want me to keep the faith and trust you, against all the evidence, but the evidence is overwhelming. My family is hounding me and strong-arming me. And there's no hard proof that I can cling to. Just a story I made up about who I think you are. And I want it to be true so damn badly, I'm afraid to trust myself. I don't know where else to turn. What else to look at."

"I always trusted you," he said.

"Don't torture me. It's not fair." Her voice was sharp. "There's nothing I'd rather do than just jump off that cliff with you, trusting that we'll figure out how to fly before we hit the ground. But I can't seem to let myself jump. I... I can't let go."

Jack tossed back the rest of his second glass of Scotch, pulled out some money and placed it on the bar, under the tumbler. "I understand." He tried to keep his voice steady. "I should never have put you in this position in the first place."

"It's not that I don't believe you," she said again. "I feel the truth, shining out of you. But I feel like I'm stuck in a tar pit."

He stood up. "I know the feeling. It's the lies, dragging you down. They can drown you, if you let them."

She winced. "Jack, please don't."

"I'll get my stuff, and check out right away."

"I'm so sorry."

The pain in her golden eyes made it worse. He backed away. "Good luck with everything, Maddie," he said. "Forever."

He headed for the elevator, trying not to run into any walls.

He'd thought that he'd suffered nine years ago, when his life fell apart. He thought he'd been through the worst. But no. His punishment wasn't over yet.

They'd saved the worst for last.

Eighteen

Ten days later

The latest Moon Cat and the Kinky Ladies tune, "Aloof Angel," was playing in Maddie's earbuds as she jogged down the street. She checked the odometer on her phone: 6.3 miles, and she still needed to go back the way she came.

She'd been out running every day, ever since that night in the bar. Trying to outrun her own misery, but misery kept pace with her like a patient shadow.

She was hiding out from the other Mosses. Her brothers had tried to console her, but the harder they tried, the worse she felt. Tilda, Ronnie, Marcus, Caleb, her friends, all of them tried.

Even little Annika had brought a batch of lemon cupcakes with pink glaze and silver sprinkles to Maddie's house, just to cheer her up.

Which was absolutely adorable, and it broke her heart. Of course, she couldn't be bad-tempered with sweet little Annika. She'd become a doting aunt to Annika as soon as Caleb had discovered that he was a father, and the connection she'd forged with the little girl had got her dreaming about motherhood. And lately, about starting a family with Jack.

She kept imagining their sweet little faces. Gifts from that timeline when she'd still thought herself able to prove that Jack was innocent. To everyone, even herself. She'd failed, and that timeline had faded into the mist, its gifts lost beyond recall.

She'd be mourning that vanished alternate life forever.

One thing was for sure. She wasn't marrying anybody else before her thirtieth birthday. Or at all, ever. MossTech was going to the dogs, and Uncle Jerome was welcome to it.

After all, Caleb, Marcus and Tilda would survive. They were talented, they had grit. They'd find other work. Found other companies.

Last week she'd written them all a formal letter

and had it couriered to their private addresses. One for Gran, one for Caleb, one for Marcus. She had informed them of her final decision not to comply with the conditions of Gran's mandate. Told them she regretted more than she could express that the consequences of that decision touched them all, not just her alone. She finished by telling them that she loved them, and was taking some time alone to think. Before they had a chance to respond, she'd shut up her house and moved into a friend's apartment. Turning off the phone. Withdrawing from social media.

It wasn't like anyone was gloating, or saying *I told you so.* Her family was too kind and decent for that. But the hushed whispers, the pitying looks, the pep talks, the endless advice…for God's sake. Enough. She was too raw to tolerate it. If she spent time with her family, she'd end up lashing out. Saying something unforgivable.

Conveniently enough, her friend Wende had left to spend six weeks in London, and had given Maddie the keys to her apartment before she left. Perfect timing. Once Wende returned, Maddie's current plan was to go to Hawaii to visit Lorena, an old college friend. Lorena had called her to conduct an audit of her accounting department. The timing was perfect, and the ticket was booked. Her trip was in two days, and she couldn't wait to climb on that plane. Though she was afraid that this sickening ache would travel with her wherever she went.

She reached the end of the park, and was sprinting down the street when she noticed the six-story office park towering on one side, the logo on the side of the building.

Ballard ChemZyne. A chemical manufacturer that had partnered with MossTech in the past. She had met Steve and Jodi Ballard. They were down-to-earth, funny, devoted to each other. Lucky them, to be able to run their professional life as a couple.

Oops, wrong train of thought. She put on a burst of speed, as Moon Cat crooned the refrain of the song into her ears.

If Aloof Angel dares to seek the bitter truths of love,
She'll find those truths are only seen from very high above,
Oh, so very high above.

At that moment, the sign outside the condo complex came into focus. Sylvan Luxury Condominiums. Oh, crap. Seriously? She was sprinting for miles through town to unload her feelings, and she ran straight to Jack's old apartment building?

Fate was jerking her around, playing dumb, malicious pranks on her.

She ran around the corner, and skidded to a halt, blocked by massive scaffolding. Restoration work was being done on the facade of the building, and the only way forward was to cross the street and go around the whole thing. Panting, she stared up at the workers as they lowered a big bucket on a rope from a third-story window, filled with chunks of broken concrete. The refrain swelled in her ears.

She'll find those truths are only seen from very high above,
Oh, so very high above.

Maddie straightened up, wiping the sweat from her forehead as her eyes followed the bucket being dragged back up. She turned around, and went around the corner, staring up at the Ballard ChemZyne building. Four stories higher than anything else around here.

A black sports car was waiting for the Sylvan Condos gate to open. Maddie started running again, timing it so that she'd run right through the gate after it.

She followed the signs to Building Six, Jack, Amelia and Gabriella's building, and walked around it, gazing up from every angle while doing glute and hamstring stretches. She thought about Amelia's apartment. One floor up. One apartment over.

That huge tree had a long, thick branch that extended in front of Jack's apartment. She thought of how the leaves had trembled and the boughs had swayed in the wind.

The tree was taller now, after nine years. Of course. She wondered if the other trees in the video had been shaking in the wind, too. She hadn't thought to check. She'd been too focused on Jack's balcony. Watching it fixedly for signs of an intruder.

Outside cameras watched the entire side of that building, but because of the tree, apartment 416 was uniquely positioned to have a small blind spot behind that tree branch, right over what must be a smaller window, since all the other apartments had a window in that position. Probably a bathroom.

In unit 416, that window could not be seen behind the thick foliage.

She looked up at Ballard ChemZyne, estimating the angles, the sight lines. There could be cameras on that building that would be able to see into that blind spot.

Damn. Now she was attracting attention. A woman who had walked out the front entrance was giving her the fish-eye. Time to stroll away and break into a jog, before anyone accused her of loitering or, God forbid, called the cops on her. She winced to think of what Caleb or Gran would say when they came to bail her out. If they came at all.

She headed toward the gate, pulling her phone out of her armband strap, and found Jodi Ballard's number.

"Hello, Jodi Ballard's office! This is Samantha speaking," chirped a young woman's voice.

"Hi. Could I speak to Jodi, please?"

"May I ask who's calling?"

"Certainly. This is Maddie Moss, from Moss-Tech."

"Oh! Okay. One moment, please."

Maddie thought of Jack's teasing about how she navigated through the world so smoothly with her magical phone calls. But it was really just that oh so magical word, MossTech. She couldn't take personal credit for that. Only Grandpa Bertram could. For Maddie, it was just an accident of her birth. But it would be stupid not to take advantage of it.

"Hello, Maddie!" Jodi Ballard's warm, friendly voice came on the line. "Great to hear from you!"

They exchanged pleasantries. Maddie got to the point as soon as politeness would allow. "This is a strange request, Jodi. But could you tell me if your security camera at the Blake Street ChemZyne offices surveils the outside of the building across from it, facing east? The Sylvan Condos complex?"

Jodi thought about it. "I assume so," she said. "I believe we have an outdoor shot of the building on every side. Why do you ask?"

"Would you still have archived security video from nine years ago?"

"Good God, I have no idea. Why do you ask?"

"This is a very long shot," Maddie said. "But do you remember what happened with BioSpark, my brother Caleb's company, and Jack Daly?"

"I certainly do," Jodi said. "Terrible business. I was so sorry about all that."

"Jack Daly lived at Sylvan Condos at the time," Maddie explained. "An email was sent from his desktop computer there that he swears he didn't send. An order to buy stock in Energen. He says he was set up, but there is no record of anyone entering his apartment that night. At least, not any that appears on the Sylvan Condos security footage. The email in question was sent at 2:10 a.m. I looked over the video from the Sylvan Condos security, and I noticed that there's a blind spot. But it wouldn't be blind from the top two floors of the Ballard ChemZyne building. And I'm wondering if there's a camera up there that might have Jack's former apartment building in its sight line."

Jodi was quiet for a moment. "What an odd request," she said. "After nine years."

"I know, I know," Maddie said. "Very strange. If it's not possible, I understand."

"Oh, I didn't mean that. I'm just thinking, well...if you had your own personal reasons for wanting to find Jack Daly innocent, let's just say, don't get your hopes up."

"Oh, I'm really not," Maddie said hastily. "No hopes. I'm just being thorough. Out of an abundance of caution. And fairness. There's certainly no reason not to look, right?"

"You're absolutely right. I'll call my security people right away," Jodi said.

"I'll leave my email with Samantha," Maddie said. "Thank you, Jodi. I appreciate you being so kind and understanding."

"I'll get back to you soon," Jodi promised. "Just the time it takes to ask them if we can help you out."

Maddie had wings on her feet for the run back to Wende's apartment. She went straight up and sat down at the table in front of her laptop, checking emails without even taking a shower first.

There was a page full of unread messages, mostly from her family, but at the top were two new ones. She clicked on the one from Jodi Ballard.

Hi, Maddie. As discussed, our security team dug up the archived video for you. Hope it helps! Keep me posted, and good luck with everything.

There was another email, from someone on Jodi's security team.

Dear Ms. Moss:
As per your request, attached is the video covering the hours of 6:00 PM to the hours of 6:00

AM on the referenced date. Please let me know if you have any trouble with the format.

She set it to play, and fast-forwarded the video to midnight, before Gabriella had left. She could widen the timeframe later if she needed to.

The first thing she noticed was that there was no wind in those trees. They were absolutely still, as the seconds on the counter ticked by. The camera showed an outdoor terrace café on the top floor, and Jack's building in the background was blurry, but still visible. The camera looked down on it from above.

Then she saw it. A dark flash, disappearing into the trees. But it wasn't Jack's balcony. It was from a floor above, and one over. Amelia's balcony.

She watched it again, slowing it down. A dark figure clambered over the railing of Amelia's balcony, and swiftly lowered himself down on a rope. He disappeared into the branches of the tree below. The branches trembled and swayed. He must be creeping along the big branch. Nothing was visible from Jack's balcony. The intruder had climbed into the bathroom window, hidden by foliage.

Which must have been left open for him by Jack's lying, traitorous fiancée.

Maddie was startled to realize that she was pressing her hands to her mouth and rocking, tears streaming down her face.

Oh, Jack. He'd been exiled from his whole world. He'd gone to prison. She herself had left him twisting in the wind, alone. And he had deserved none of it. None.

She felt ashamed of herself, but she kept watching in helpless fascination.

Sixteen minutes later in the video, the tree bough started to shake. Shortly afterward, the dark figure swiftly and athletically climbed the rope back up to Amelia's balcony. He pulled the rope up after himself, and disappeared inside.

The whole thing had been invisible from below.

They had framed Jack. Smoothly, expertly. Who would do that to a decent, hardworking man? What the hell was in their heads? She would never understand.

Her phone buzzed. It was Jodi Ballard. She hit Talk. "Hi, Jodi."

"Did you just see what I just saw?" Jody sounded awestruck.

"You watched the video?" Maddie said.

"Yeah, Steve and I are home right now, watching it together. Oh, my God, Maddie. This changes everything, doesn't it?"

"Yes." Her voice broke. "Yes, it absolutely does."

"Oh, honey," Jodi said. "Do you need someone with you? I could come over."

"I'll be fine," Maddie whispered. "Thanks, Jodi."

"Will you share this info with the police, or should we?"

"I'll make sure that it gets to the detective who handled the case," Maddie assured her. "That'll be my next phone call. I'll let you know when it's done."

"Great. But we'll be more than happy to help, if they contact us directly. Oh, Maddie, this is just huge. I want to tell everyone. Oh, wait a minute. We can tell people about this, can't we?"

"Why not?" Maddie said. "You guys shot that video. You own it. Tell anyone you want. Tell everyone, Jodi. The more people who know, the better it is for Jack."

"Music to my ears," Jodi said jubilantly. "It's the juiciest gossip I ever got to spread, and it's positive, so my conscience can be clear. I never really thought Jack Daly was a crook, you know? It just felt wrong to me. Just off somehow."

"That's great, Jodi," Maddie said. "Spread it abroad. To everyone you can."

"Thank you for bringing this to our attention," Jodi said. "A great injustice has been done, and it's high time that it was put right. I'm so glad to help with that."

"I couldn't agree more," Maddie said.

She got off the phone, still feeling dazed. The rehabilitation of Jack Daly's reputation had already begun. Jodi knew everyone in the tech business world, and she loved to talk. It couldn't be better.

Maddie sat there, staring into space. Then she shook herself into movement, and composed an email to her brother, attaching the video footage from Ballard ChemZyne.

Caleb, you were wrong about Jack. Attached is security video of the night the Energen order was placed, shot from the top of Ballard ChemZyne. Fast forward to 2:05 a.m. The intruder climbed down from Amelia Howard's apartment, and into Jack's bathroom window. Once you've watched, please contact Detective Stedman, and send the video to him immediately.
Maddie.

She sent the email, shaking with emotion. After about twenty minutes, her phone rang. The display showed Caleb's name.

She picked up. "Did you see the video?" she demanded.

"Maddie... I don't know what to say." Caleb sounded as dazed as she felt.

"I can think of a few things you can say. To Jack, anyway. Did you tell Gran?"

"Yes. She can hardly believe—"

"Show her the video. She has to believe it if it's right in her face."

"Maddie, this doesn't necessarily answer all of the questions—"

"It answers enough of them," she said. "Amelia lived in that apartment above Jack's. Greer was sleeping with Amelia, in order to have access to her apartment. He drugged her that night. She lost consciousness after drinking wine he'd brought. Gabriella must have drugged Jack, too, and while he was unconscious, she entered his password into his computer and opened that bathroom window for Greer. Then she left, and went to the nightclub to establish her own alibi while Greer did her dirty work. They made Jack their scapegoat. And everyone fell for it. Even his best friend." She swallowed. "Even me," she finished, in a whisper.

"Don't scold me. I'm blown away by this, too."

"Yeah, right. Did you call Stedman?"

"Of course. I sent him the video. He's reviewing it now."

"Call Jack," she said forcefully.

"Maddie, I—"

"Call him. Now. I just sent you his contact info. You owe him that, Caleb. Tell him you know the truth. It'll mean the world to him."

"Why not tell him yourself? I'm sure he'd rather hear this from you."

"No, he wouldn't." Maddie's voice caught. "He won't want to talk to me. I left him high and dry, after you guys worked me over. I displayed absolutely no backbone at all. He's never going to want to see me again. And I don't blame him. Not one little bit."

"Maddie, that's ridiculous," Caleb said brusquely. "Would you just tell us where the hell you are, so that we can talk about this like adults?"

"I don't feel particularly adult right now. Goodbye, Caleb."

She ended the call, and pulled up the number for the car service. "Hello?" she said, when they picked up. "This is Maddie Moss. I want a car to take me to the airport in one hour." She rattled off the address, and hung up.

She wasn't waiting for her flight to Hawaii in two days. Her work here was done, and she was riding off into the sunset right now. Starting the next phase in her life, however bleak. She'd missed out on earthly paradise—out of cowardice. She'd burned all her bridges. The ones that led to the only place on earth that she wanted to be.

In Jack Daly's arms.

Nineteen

The coffee had gone stone-cold.

This had been happening way too often. He'd get himself a fresh cup, sit down to stare at raindrops sliding down the slanted skylights of the Cleland forest house, or dripping slowly off the ferns outside. After an hour or two, he'd look down at the cup. Cold, again.

He'd turned off the phone ringer a while ago. It was too much. All the noise and furor, people talking too loudly. Everyone he'd ever known, trying to hunt him down to assure him that they'd always been sure he was innocent.

Had they, now. He wished he could believe it. He wished even more that he could enjoy it.

Everything he'd dreamed of all these years, finally happening. But it gave him no satisfaction. Because the one phone call or message that he craved never arrived, and he couldn't seem to stop waiting for it. Hoping for it.

Maddie had cleared his name, rehabilitated his reputation with one brilliant stroke of her usual genius, let the whole world know about his changed status, and vanished.

Jack poured the coffee down the sink, and briefly considered trying again, but why bother? Sometimes, a man just needed to learn when to quit.

He activated the computer screen, and scrolled numbly through pages of unread email messages. Some from Detective Stedman. Most from former business associates who had shunned him after the BioSpark disaster, and were now all excited to be his friend again. Very touching. Useful, too. It would help in building back his career. He guessed.

But he just wasn't ready to make nice yet.

Elaine Moss had sent him a stiffly worded but sincere handwritten letter of apology on embossed MossTech letterhead, and he'd appreciated that communication more than all of the "I never doubted you" emails. Elaine was no bullshitter. She had the guts to admit when she'd been wrong, and she wanted to make amends. He respected that.

His heart revved when he heard a car engine outside, and he lunged for the window. Not Maddie's Mini Cooper. This was a black Porsche, one he did not recognize.

It pulled to a stop. Caleb Moss got out.

Jack observed himself as if he were outside of his own body as a complicated rush of emotions boiled up inside him. Disappointment. Anger. Hurt. Confusion.

And hope.

Caleb stood by his car and waited, not approaching the house. He'd seen Jack watching him through the window.

Jack took a deep breath, and went to the front door. Opened it.

They stared at each other. Rain was pelting down, and the air was heavy and sweet from the damp, fragrant earth.

Caleb made no move to shield himself from the rain. He just stood there, silently waiting for Jack's invitation.

Aw, screw it. Jack beckoned wearily. "Come on in. You're getting soaked."

Caleb followed him in. "Great place," he said. "I love the canyon and the creek."

"It's just a vacation rental, but I really like it," Jack said. "I keep coming back here. It's worth the long drive to the city."

"Yeah." They stood staring at each other. Jack forced himself to break the spell, waving him toward a chair. "Sit down," he said. "I'll make us some fresh coffee."

Caleb sat down at the table while he got to work. This time around, Jack was in no danger of zoning out as he scooped the coffee. The air sang with nail-biting tension.

"You wouldn't answer my calls," Caleb said. "Or my emails."

Jack set it to brew and sat down at the table. "Lots to process," he said. "It's been a weird week."

"I bet it has," Caleb said. "So it's all out in the open, now that Bill Greer and Gabriella Adriana confessed. The papers are full of it, you know? There's a long article in *Time*, in *Wired*. One in *The Economist*, too. Did you read them?"

"No," Jack said.

"They say that LeBlanc has admitted to stealing our research. The whole industry is in an uproar. It's a legal nightmare."

"I'm sure it'll all shake out eventually."

"Crazy, how long they planned this thing. And Greer? What an asshole. Getting involved with that woman just to drug her and use her apartment. Gabriella, too. What a piece of work. So calculated."

"And the whole time, she was sleeping in my bed." Jack's voice was dull. "We were talking marriage, while she plotted to destroy me. So much for my powers of perception. I don't have much judgment when it comes to women."

"Oh, I don't know," Caleb said, his voice carefully neutral. "Maddie was a prize."

Jack shrugged. "Well, she's not here, is she?"

"No, but it's complicated. And I didn't help with that—"

"You most certainly did not help with that," Jack broke in. "But I don't blame you. At least, not for that part of it. If she'd been my sister, I would've done the same."

"I appreciate your understanding," Caleb said. "Have you gotten in touch with her?"

Jack did a double take. "Why would I? She walked away. She never called back. What could I possibly say to her?"

"Oh, *thank you*, maybe?" Caleb's voice rang out. "For not giving up? For flogging away until she found the truth? That's more than anyone else did. Even you."

Jack couldn't seem to stop shaking his head. "Of course I want to follow her. But I can't force myself on her. I don't want to be that pathetic bad news boyfriend that hangs on like a tick even when things are over."

"You aren't," Caleb told him. "Maddie thinks it's you who doesn't want her."

Jack jolted upright. "What? She said that?"

"She said, 'I left him high and dry, after you guys worked me over. He'll never want to see me again.' Her exact words."

Jack's mouth worked. "But I...but she..."

"You already let Gabriella and her merry band of thieves knock a hole in your life," Caleb said. "Don't miss out on Maddie, too, just because you're chickenshit."

The coffee gurgled. Jack was too dazed by Caleb's revelation to take offense. He got up, pouring fresh coffee into their mugs. "Wait. Are you sure she said that? Those exact words? You're not jerking me around?"

"I'm sure," Caleb said. "You got Gran's letter, I take it?"

"Yes," Jack said. "And I appreciated it. I intend

to send a reply as soon as I get my brain back online."

"It's simpler if you come in person. Come to dinner. We all want to see you."

"All?" He looked up, staring directly into Caleb's eyes.

"I can only speak for me, Gran, Tilda, Marcus and Ronnie," Caleb admitted. "Maddie's gone AWOL. We have no idea where she is."

"Gone?" That gave him a nasty jolt. "What do you mean, gone? Like, missing?"

"No, not missing," Caleb assured him. "She just doesn't want to be bothered with us. She's done this before, when she gets sick of family drama. She takes off and sends us snarky little messages, letting us know she's fine, telling us to get over ourselves and leave her the hell alone. Like she did during that week she spent with you."

"So you have absolutely no idea where she is," Jack said.

Caleb shook his head. "Actually, I was hoping she'd said something to you."

Jack set his coffee down with a thud. "No," he said. "She hasn't gotten in touch."

Caleb's phone buzzed. He pulled it out. "It's

Ronnie. Give me just a second." He accepted the video call. "Hey Ron. What's up?"

"Caleb! I'm glad you picked up!" Ronnie sounded excited. "I have news!"

"Great," Caleb said. "I'm up here in Cleland, talking to Jack."

"Yeah? Wow. Give him my best. Better yet, put the phone where I can see him."

Caleb held up the phone between them before Jack had a chance to shrink out of sight, and he was waving at Veronica Moss, who was outdoors someplace sunny, the wind whipping her long red hair around her head. "Hey, Ronnie," he said.

"Jack," she said. "I'm really glad about what happened."

"Thanks," he said.

"And I'm sorry for what I said to you, at Ava's wedding."

"It's all right," Jack said. "To be honest, in all the excitement, I barely noticed it."

"Okay. I really mean it, though. Pass me back to Caleb. I have news for him."

Caleb turned the phone around toward himself. "What news?" he asked.

"I got a video call from Maddie," Ronnie announced.

Jack's ears pricked up.

"Did she say where she was?" Caleb asked.

"No, but I recognized the place!" Ronnie's voice vibrated with excitement. "She was on the beach when she called, and when she turned around, I recognized the hotel behind her. It was the Royal Embassy Suites, in Honolulu. I stayed there with Jareth last winter."

"That makes sense," Caleb said. "She mentioned that her friend Lorena wanted her to do a consulting job in Hawaii. Good detective work, Ron."

"You bet. Shall we go look for her together? You, me and Marcus?"

"No," Jack broke in. "Stay here. I'll go to Hawaii. The rest of you guys can stay the hell out of my way for once. You owe me that."

Caleb and Ronnie were both startled into silence. Nervous seconds ticked by.

"Uh, right," Caleb said carefully. "Ron, call you later, okay?"

"You better believe you will," she replied.

Caleb ended the call and slid his phone into his pocket.

"So?" Jack said. "I don't want to trip over you guys. I need space for this."

"Will you take off right now?" Caleb asked.

"As soon as you leave," Jack said.

Caleb let out a bark of laughter. "So in other words, don't let the door hit your ass on the way out."

"My life in recent years hasn't polished up my manners," he said, unrepentant.

"Fine, fine. Go to Hawaii. We all wish you luck. Just promise me that you'll message me the second that you find her, so we can all breathe easier, especially Gran."

"I can do that," Jack promised. "I'll see you out."

Caleb cast a bemused look over his shoulder as Jack herded him out the door.

"What's next for you, Jack?" he asked.

"That depends on Maddie," Jack said.

"I mean professionally," Caleb specified.

"That also depends on Maddie," Jack told him. "If it's a no, I'll probably leave the country. Go trek in the Himalayas. Eat lentils and grow my beard down to my waist. Join the French Foreign Legion. Who cares. I certainly won't."

"I know you're anxious to go, but just so it's out there. I've heard about your new super-enzyme project," Caleb said. "Word's gotten around. And MossTech is interested."

"No kidding." Jack was startled.

"You might not want to partner with Moss-

Tech, since as you know, the company is in flux. And since Maddie has officially blown up Gran's plot to marry us all off, I'll soon be out of a job myself. Uncle Jerome will fire Marcus and Tilda and me. I just want you to know that I'm interested in partnering with you again."

Jack stopped on the stone walkway outside. "Really? After everything that went down between us, you want to reboot BioSpark?"

Caleb turned around, and nodded. "I've never worked with anyone with a mind like yours," he said. "Except for Tilda. She's in your league. With the two of you, we could go for world domination. Plus, I just miss my best friend." His jaw was tight, a muscle pulsing in his cheek. "I get that you're pissed," he said, his voice halting. "I know that actions have consequences. If you want me to leave you the hell alone, I'll understand. But that's what I would want. In my perfect, ideal world. Think about it."

Jack was barely aware of the rain plastering his hair to his forehead. "I am still pissed," he admitted. "But I missed you, too. I missed our brain-meld."

"Me, too," Caleb said.

"But if Maddie cuts me loose, I'm out of here,"

Jack told him. "As far across the world as I can go without coming back the other way."

"Understood." Caleb pulled open the door and got into his car. "But you'll be going with my friendship, and my apology. If you'll accept it. Good luck."

"Thanks," Jack replied.

The window hummed up, and Caleb's car started up and drove away.

Jack went inside, still dazed, and sat down at the computer to check flights to Honolulu. There was one that took off in about four hours, that he might make if he was lucky, and hit no traffic.

He threw some stuff haphazardly into a bag, grabbed his passport and hit the road. There was no time to waste, but even so, on his way through Cleland, he hit the brakes so hard in front of the jewelry store, the car fishtailed on the rain-slicked asphalt.

He burst into the shop. "Hey. A couple of weeks ago, I was looking at engagement rings with my girlfriend," he told the saleswoman, already fishing out his credit card. "There was a sapphire and ruby ring in a thick white gold band. Is it still available?"

"I do believe that it is!" the woman said, with a big smile. "I'll go check."

Jack stared at the seconds ticking by as he waited for her. He was desperate to get on that plane, but by God, he would be completely equipped for this encounter first.

As equipped as a man head-over-ass in love could possibly be.

Twenty

Maddie walked through the churning foam, letting the rush of the surf soothe her ears. It was the only thing that helped her breathe. Otherwise, the air stuck somewhere around her breastbone in a lump, burning and cramping.

She'd worked nonstop on Lorena's project, keeping too busy to think or feel. But today, she'd wrapped it up and presented her friend with a complete analysis, so the rest of the day stretched out, long and dull and empty. Sort of like her whole life.

She'd put on a light, gauzy dress that floated at knee length, and headed off for a walk along the beach. She had to keep moving, or she'd drown in these feelings.

She'd followed the story in the press. Bit by bit, the sordid tale of how Gabriella, Greer and LeBlanc had set Jack up emerged. Some articles had pictures of Jack, but they were old, from before the BioSpark scandal. In all accounts, Jack Daly was "unavailable for comment."

He wasn't in the mood to indulge anybody's curiosity. She could relate.

Now that Lorena's job was done, she had to come up with a plan. She had plenty of job offers. Maybe she could just keep bouncing from job to job forever. It was as good a plan as any, and had the advantage of keeping her a step ahead of her inquisitive family.

But the work didn't satisfy her anymore. The fun factor was gone.

Maybe fun and thrills were too much to ask of an adult working life. Maybe they always had been, and she'd been childish and unrealistic all along. Time to face reality.

So freaking much reality. It made her tired. Day after day of it. Dull and flat.

"Maddie."

The sound of Jack's voice behind her made her

freeze, heart galloping. She didn't look around. She must be imagining this.

She turned slowly, and air whooshed out of her lungs, leaving her light-headed.

Jack stood there, barefoot in the surf. His soul in his eyes.

"Jack?" Her voice shook. "What are you doing here? How did you find me?"

"Ronnie recognized the hotel behind you in the video call."

"Oh," Maddie said. "So you're in cahoots with my family? That's weird."

"No, just using any resource available to me," he said. "I needed to see you."

"For what?" she asked.

"To thank you," he said. "For clearing my name."

Maddie bit her lip. The look on his face was making her confused. Almost as if—but no. She didn't dare to hope. She wouldn't survive being disappointed again.

"You're welcome," she said stiffly. "It seemed like the least that I could do."

"The least that you can do is a whole lot better than everybody else's best," he said. He stepped toward her, his eyes pleading. "Please, Maddie."

"Please, what?" Water swirled, tugging at the

bottom of her skirt. "I fulfilled our bargain. Your name is cleared, your enemies are brought low, you have your friends back, career possibilities open to you. What are you complaining about?"

"I don't have you," he said. "Without you, the rest is worth nothing."

Her eyes filled, to her dismay. "I didn't think you wanted that." Her voice quavered. "Not after that night. I let Gabriella and Greer and my folks shake my faith in you. I knew you felt betrayed. And I was so sorry. But I can't take it back."

"Don't be sorry," he said. "I was framed by experts. They fooled the police, too. How could you not be shaken? You're trained to look at facts and draw conclusions, not to make wild leaps of faith and hope it'll turn out okay. I don't blame you for being confused. Particularly not after you saved my ass by hunting down that video."

She still stood there, shaking. Eyes full. Speechless.

Jack took her hand. "Babe," he said gently. "The tide's coming in. You're going to get soaked. Or knocked over."

"You're not angry?" she whispered.

"Are you kidding?" He tugged her hand. "You put me to shame, Maddie. I flounced off to sulk in the dark, and you went off to nail those dirty bastards for me all by yourself. Why did you even bother helping me, after I behaved like that?"

She looked at her hand, cradled in his. "It was the right thing to do," she said. "You have important work to do. The world needs it. I wasn't going to let a greedy, snotty hag like Gabriella stomp all over that with her spike heels. Much less that muscle-headed goon who does her dirty work. I hope they both enjoy prison."

"Me, too," Jack said. "So you just helped me on principle?"

"No." Maddie's voice felt unsteady. "I just wanted you to have a shot at being happy. I thought, if I could give you that, it would be some small satisfaction."

"Why stop at small satisfactions?" he asked. "Let's go for the big ones. All of the amazing things that life could offer us. I want them with you, Maddie. Only with you."

"Oh, Jack." Her throat was quivering. She felt out of control.

"I love you," Jack said roughly. "You are an astonishing woman. Fascinating, brilliant, mysterious. I want to spend my life giving you satisfaction. Every day. Every night." He reached into his pocket, pulled out a ring box and opened it.

It was the ring she'd fallen in love with back at the jewelers in Cleland. So much had happened since then. "Oh, my God, Jack," she breathed. "It's my ring."

His face lit up. "That sounds promising. Yes, it is your ring, and I hope you'll wear it. Maddie Moss, will you be my wife? Will you let me love you forever?"

She dug for a tissue, and mopped her nose. "Yes," she said brokenly. "Yes."

Jack was so beautiful when he grinned, with those sexy lines around his eyes all crinkled up. His face shone with joy as he slid the ring onto her finger and kissed her knuckles. They melted into each other's arms.

Sometime later, he lifted his head. "Hey. It occurs to me that if we get married now, we'll be playing into your gran's hands. Do you want to encourage her like this?"

Maddie's laughter felt free and happy. "Shall we pass this hot potato to Marcus, and watch him squirm?" she mused. "I bet he was so relieved to be off the hook, even if it meant that he was also out of a job. It could be very entertaining. Let's think about it."

"All I can think about is you," Jack said. "This timeline, the one where you and I get our crap figured out just in time, and latch on to each other for all eternity."

"Yes." She hugged him again, burying her face against his chest. "Isn't it funny? It all started for us at the beach, with our feet in the surf. And here we are again."

The surf swirled and churned wildly around their feet as they kissed. But they stood together, as solid and steady as a rock.

* * * * *

LET'S TALK

Romance

For exclusive extracts, competitions
and special offers, find us online:

f facebook.com/millsandboon

⬡ @millsandboonuk

y @millsandboon

Or get in touch on 0844 844 1351*

For all the latest titles coming soon,
visit millsandboon.co.uk/nextmonth

*Calls cost 7p per minute plus your phone company's price per
minute access charge

Want even more
ROMANCE?

Join our bookclub today!

'Mills & Boon books, the perfect way to escape for an hour or so.'

Miss W. Dyer

'Excellent service, promptly delivered and very good subscription choices.'

Miss A. Pearson

'You get fantastic special offers and the chance to get books before they hit the shops'

Mrs V. Hall